I0739610

The Emerald Door

Megan E. Vaughn

FSF Publications

Cover art and design by KAD Creations
ISBN 978-0-9961485-0-4
ISBN 978-0-9961485-1-1
Manufactured in the United States of America.
FIRST Edition
First US Printing: 2015
www.fivesmilingfish.com

This book is dedicated:
To my parents and my brother, for caring for and simultaneously warping my mind.
To Danielle, Betsy, and Shannon for putting up with me since kindergarten.
To Jenn and Jeff for not laughing when I fell off the couch. . .oh wait, yes you did!
To Will, May, Misty, and Holly for all those times I poked you in the arm and you didn't kill me.
To Amber, Parker, and Audrey for the little things, the big things, and the things in-between that tend to fall between the couch cushions.
To that one guy with face and the teeth. . .the one I saw that movie with that one time. That was a good time.
And to Kira Shay and Sidney Reetz for all of the support, the swearing, the suppers, and the spell checking.

Chapter One:
The First Floor; Remembering the Storm

Dory used to live in a gorgeous loft apartment in one of the nicer neighborhoods of the busy city. The building was called Kansas Heights and was full of state-of-the-art security measures, not to mention free cable. Everything within was modern, sleek, and stylish. The color scheme was bright and warm with no fancy décor or added flourish to the trim. The design was sensible and practical yet still beautiful in its architectural simplicity. The single bedroom home she occupied barely fit into her budget. Still, scrimping and saving was worth it for the fireplace, over a thousand square feet, and picture window overlooking the park. Plus, no horrible neighbors or building bullies.

She'd had her share of cowering towards men who stole her newspaper or old women that barked at single moms for their kids running in the hallway. Kansas Heights had none of that. Most people kept to themselves and that was the way Dory liked things. She had her own problems without having other people adding to them.

Then the storm came.

Dory remembered getting off the bus and seeing the darkened sky. The wind had nearly knocked her over as she ran towards the building door. She stepped through the threshold of her apartment just in time for a siren to sound signaling the storm's presence. The sound caused her puppy, a Goldendoodle her parents had given her, to burst into a fit of hysterics. He howled as she pulled him into the safety of her arms.

"Frank, you're not helping," she grumbled to him in a soothing tone.

Over the course of three hours, the storm shattered the windows, flooded the floor, and tore her beloved apartment to pieces. As instructed by security, Dory and Frank hid in the basement with her neighbors. She listened to the building overhead being nearly destroyed. Wood and metal beat against each other. Dirt and mold wafted on the air as the clouds burst, pouring water over the outside world. The other tenants all waited in their respective corners, none of them trying to console each other outside of their own families. When the lightning would flicker in the high basement windows, Dory could see that each person wore the same horrified expression, children and adult alike.

For the first time, Dory wished they were sociable; that she had someone to talk to in order to drown out the sound of wind, rain, and breaking glass. She made lists in her head of things she had done with her life. She'd finished college, taken road trips with friends, dated, and she even had a good relationship with her parents. If the storm got worse, would she be ready to die?

Instantly, Dory caught her own thoughts. "Damn it, I'm depressed," she muttered. Her dog whimpered in response.

Crashing and thrashing overhead made several of the people jump and pull their children closer. Dory wondered if she turned to one of those mothers and said hello, would they would continue the conversation? She wondered if the small talk would distract her from the fear churning in her stomach each time the wind beat against the ceiling. If she invited the kids to pet her dog would it calm their crying?

One family in particular caught her eye. A mother in

her late twenties had baby curled up in her lap and a six year old grasping her side. Both of her arms enveloped her children as she hummed softly. Dory thought of speaking as she inspected them. The baby shook a teething ring with jerky, fretful motions. A picture book leaned awkwardly against the side of the six year old called "Monster Tea Party" where a vampire, werewolf, and ghost stared out at a Dory with goofy grins. Instead of taking comfort in small talk, Dory hugged Frank to her until the storm passed.

Firemen came to help them out of the basement, but their home was no longer livable. Dory couldn't even manage an upturn of her mouth at the square jawed man in yellow who took her hand as she emerged from the world below.

"Are you alright, miss?" The fireman offered her a gorgeous, concerned smile and gave her hand a reassuring squeeze.

Dory did not have an answer. She stared at the building from the sidewalk where paramedics were quickly checking over each of the people with flashlights and a list of questions about their well-being. A couple of walls had been partially reduced to chunks of concrete. The flat roof had caved in, turning the top floor into a pancake. Kansas Heights had been decimated, leaving dozens of people to find new homes while it was repaired.

The Optical Zenith Apartment building was the only place with an available space along a bus route to Dory's work. The neighborhood appeared to be safe and it was cheaper than Kansas Heights. Her father had found an advertisement for it in the newspaper and her mother made the call while Dory was collecting the remnants of her former home.

Coming back to her parents' house, her father pushed the newspaper ad in front of her with a little shrug. He then lifted Frank as if his part in the search was over and therefore it was time for him to play with the dog.

"It's a one bedroom on the first floor," her mother stated as Dory eyed the block print suspiciously.

"Do I have any other choice?" Dory muttered. She couldn't stay with her parents without spending the majority of her paycheck on the commute into the city. "I should petition that the government should help re-build Kansas Heights. After all, it was their job to make sure the building was up to code and able to withstand acts of nature."

Her mom gave a patronizing laugh. "Yes dear, but you'll still need someplace to live. We can help you finish packing tomorrow. When I called, they told me you can move in as soon as you want." Dory knew her mother was sympathetic; still there was no way she could know the full tragedy of such a loss like Kansas Heights.

"It's just for a few months," Dory rationalized to her parents. "I won't be living there forever. Before I know it, I'll be back in Kansas Heights and out of . . . What did you say the name of this place was?"

"Optical Zenith Apartments on Desert Street," her father told her, glancing up from Frank who was sitting on his haunches, begging for a treat.

"Wow, what a dumb name," she commented.

The next day she viewed the apartment, then made preparations with her folks to have her possessions relocated by the following week. She would have to use precious vacation time to settle in.

On the day after she moved in, Dory's chest felt heavy with frustration. Waking had been a long process; it was as if she were afraid that crawling out of bed would remind her that she was no longer in her home. Dory did at last roll onto the floor, nearly hitting Frank's rarely used dog bed. The puppy was snoring peacefully upon her mattress in a nest he had made from her comforter.

Standing and kicking at the hem of her pajama pants, Dory groaned loudly at her new apartment. Looking disdainfully down at the metal furnace under the dirty bedroom window, she remembered her old fireplace longingly. The wooden floor was littered with her things. She knew that unpacking should be her first priority, yet the sight of the tiny new home was enough to break her into a fit of tears. One box had spilled onto the floor in the night, letters and important papers spread like a rug beside her bed. Leaning over to scoop the contents back into their cardboard container, Dory noticed a greeting card from last year at the top of the pile. The outside had a picture of a chimpanzee with a voice bubble over his head reading "Go ape on your birthday". Inside was a quick, impersonal note from her friend Maud.

The first thought that crossed Dory's mind was how she had not seen Maud since her former college roommate had moved to Atlanta. Then again, she had barely spoken to her either. Most of Dory's friends were always "too busy" to return her calls. Her birthday had passed a month ago and Maud had yet to send a new card despite the fact that Dory had sent flowers for Maud's birthday. With a bitter, "Hmph" Dory discarded the monkey card back into the box, then kicked the box under the bed.

After another throaty noise of anger, Dory grumbled to herself, "I need to get out." Pulling open her front door, and then locking it behind her, Dory decided that a jog would be the best way to wake up. In her old neighborhood, there had been an early morning rush brought on by people trying to live a healthy lifestyle or just out walking their dogs. Normally, she would have pulled on a pair of yoga pants and her tennis shoes, wanting to blend in with the traffic. But that first morning at Optical Zenith, she didn't bother to change out of her pajama bottoms, not caring as the people leaving in their cars for work stared at her bunny slippers.

The morning air flowed through her brown hair and filled her lungs with a crisp feeling. Her slippers scraped against the rough cement, slowing her down as the floppy ears of the two gray rabbits bounced erratically. Through the minutes of her jog, she forgot about the new apartment, the fact that her whole family now lived an hour away, and that a terrible storm had demolished half of her worldly processions. Then as she rounded the corner, passing a quaint city park, the Optical Zenith Apartment building came into view once again.

The building was tall, ominous in its old fashioned nineteen-twenties design with long thin windows and shapes carved into the brickwork. Even the glass was old with long lines formed from decades of weather and grime. When the sunlight ran across it the right way, Dory swore she saw eyes watching her. In the third floor window, she imagined a pale man's face studying her intently. The idea left her again in a blink.

Either side of the stoop was guarded by two pillars with stone ravens upon the tops, their wings outstretched and their beaks open as if crying out. Dory stuck her tongue out at one as she fumbled with her key in the front door.

She never counted the floors of the building, but she heard someone mention there being twelve. From what she saw, the building couldn't possibly be that tall. There was no elevator, making her feel sorry for the people on the top floor. Staircases zigzagged throughout the building like a Jacob's ladder. The mail boxes within the foyer were comprised of little brass doors on a wall opposite a design that looked like a fake entry painted purely as decoration.

"Nice," she muttered as she glanced back outside at the raven statues. "I'm living in Boris Karloff's house."

"Well, that's too bad." A man's voice hovered behind her in the vestibule. She spun around to face him, hoping that it would turn out he was speaking on a phone and not to her. No such luck. He was boringly handsome like a model in a clothing catalog, yet Dory admitted to herself that her eyes took in every inch of him. Not a single blonde hair was out of place nor a speck of morning dust upset his tailored business suit. Despite being in his early thirties, the man had obviously done well for himself in whatever profession he'd chosen to pursue. His flaws were subtle and the result of some kind of sickness. Dark semi-circles had begun to paint his paling complexion beneath his eyes and along his cheekbones.

"What's too bad?" She rubbed the back of one leg with a bunny slipper and awkwardly tilted.

When he spoke a second time, Dory could hear the gravel of a bronchial infection. "Too bad that you're so cute, but obviously crazy. Why are you talking to yourself?"

After two or three blinks, the spell of his good looks shattered. She attempted to walk away without responding. He put an arm up to block her, his whole body moving uncomfortably into her space.

"I mean, I know all women are crazy, but—" He paused to cough into the sleeve of his suit jacket. Dory winced and made another escape attempt. His right shoulder moved further into her path. "But talking to yourself could get you locked away."

"So could harassment." He hacked out a laugh which turned into a long, dry wheeze. "Shouldn't you be going to a doctor for that?"

"You sound as bad as my boss. Crazy and paranoid. Whatever will I do with you?" Dory opened her mouth, ready to retort with a bold "How about leaving me alone?" when suddenly his face moved down near hers. She could feel the warmth radiating from his rising fever, yet illness did not slow him down. "Then again, I hear the crazy ones can also be the wild ones. Is that true?"

She elbowed him. The action had little force behind it and really just caught the man off-guard more than anything else. With another burst of coughing, he doubled over and Dory made a swift escape.

She scampered back into her residence on the first floor of the building, feeling a little like a jittery animal. With the door safely bolted, she chose to forget the man. He was not worth her time and she wouldn't be living there long enough for him to be a problem.

She had a new apartment to worry about. It overlooked the busy street. The police sirens and honking horns had seeped through the panes all night. The kitchen was literally a rectangle of tile at one end of the family room with an oven, sink, and a refrigerator. There wasn't even a counter to separate the tile from the carpet. Her chipped and worn table was set alongside the kitchen as a makeshift barrier. The bedroom had a proper door but the hinges squeaked like a crying child. A grimy film painted the world like a sepia tone photograph through the bedroom window. She worried over the stains on the carpet and she wondered what could have happened that the bar in the closet was broken off the wall.

"Frank, I'm home . . . such as it is," she yelled to the puppy that jumped out from a pile of newspaper he'd been shredding. He sat obediently at her feet with a sheet of paper still hanging from between his teeth. She giggled at him and pried the torn paper from his muzzle. "You goofy boy," she cooed at him. At least she had something around to make her smile.

"Where to start?" she asked Frank as she surveyed the room around her. Dory stood amongst the stacks of boxes, each one labeled in permanent marker with words like "kitchen torture utensils", "bedroom miscellaneous", and "tomes of mystery and other books".

Her father pointed out maybe so many things being

destroyed in the storm was a great thing as there was less to move. The statement did not cheer Dory up, but she silently admitted that having less to unpack was indeed nice. No matter what, him pointing out her lack of personal belongings was nicer than the many times her dad grumbled, "I thought you had friends to move all of this stuff?"

She started to un-stack the columns of cardboard surrounding her in search of a box of clothing. At last she found a group of boxes containing jeans, tops, and shoes. She found a button up shirt made of thin, blue and white flannel. The top three buttons were missing, but at least it did not need ironing. After dressing, she pulled on a pair of wedges in order to reach the towers of boxes. Her construction worker dad had stacked the boxes too high, always itching for the chance to build something tall.

As she shoved another cardboard square, it tumbled to the floor and collided with the wall. Something clattered within a grate. Instead of the stainless steel vents Dory was used to, her new home had black iron vent covers deigned with the same 1920s pattern as the lobby. She peered into the grate to find the source of the clang. Reaching her hand through the holes, Dory checked for loose screws. "Just what I need. I bet the air conditioning is on the fritz." Thinking she was speaking to him, Frank waddled over to stare at the vent with her.

Her fingers slipped over something cool and smooth. She managed to loop a part of the object over her index finger and pulled. Out came a key which shone as if newly polished. The clean gray color reminded Dory of silver. The teeth were squared, not jagged like her apartment key. The design was old fashioned, heavy, and unique like a key from the early 1900s.

Curiosity overtook her. Dory hopped off the floor holding the key in front of her like a flashlight in the darkness. The next half an hour was spent trying the silver object in every cupboard and closet door, but the petite mold did not fit in a single lock. She slipped it into her pocket, feeling quite important with the antique mystery close to her.

Her lease lay sprawled across the dinner table under an abandoned glass of cherry soda from the night before. Dory lifted the cup and the document rolled up within itself. Smoothing the paper back out, Dory absentmindedly glanced over the official looking wording of her latest lease. Then, a number and a single word leapt from the paper to make her gasp. Instead of the three months she had remembered agreeing upon over the phone, the contract read "for the period of three years".

"Years!" Dory shouted, catching the attention of Frank who seemed to think the word "years" meant "walk" because he headed directly to the front door. Years meant breaking a lease when she was ready to go. Years meant more paperwork and money. The single word years terrified her and she would never be able to finish unpacking with such a cloud hovering over her.

Joining Frank at the door, she commented, "I guess you want to come, huh. Let's go see who we can talk to about this." She opened the front door and the dog ran out into the hall. He settled in the middle of the floor to wait for her to lock the apartment behind them.

Dory sauntered down the long hallway, tapping on each door. No one appeared to be home and she dreaded running into the man from the lobby again. However, the offensive word from the lease gnawed at her. With Frank leading the way, she decided to try the next floor.

Chapter Two:
The Second Floor; A Council with the Cats

Dory wandered up the stairs with an annoyed grumble. "Years! I'm not living here for three years! Why would anyone live here for three years?" She paused at the top to wait for Frank who took the steps slowly. He reached out each paw as far out in front of him as he could, held it in the air for a second, hesitating before hopping to the next step. As he started to approach the fourth step, Dory lost patience. "C'mon slowpoke."

She jogged back down the steps, scooped the little dog into her arms, and took the stairs two at a time on the way back up. The second floor only held two apartments. The entrances to these homes mimicked the facade of the building with brass handles and 1920s art deco patterns etched into the wood.

Shifting the dog in her arms, Dory rapped her knuckles against apartment 2B. She heard shuffling and high pitched muttering approach the door. The voice cooed, "Who could that be, my lovelies?" The door was opened and a woman in her late sixties answered with a wide smile. She wore a flower print smock over her loosely cut beige dress. A fuzzy cat toy on a plastic stick hung out of one of the apron pockets the way a carpenter might hang his hammer on his overalls.

Dory had always been cautious with new people. Ever since her high school graduation, she learned to fear people she did not want around attaching themselves to her. This mostly came from a long history of lousy friendships and needy boyfriends.

Her tone to the woman was alert and formal. "Hi, sorry to bother you. I'm Dorothea. I just moved into the apartment directly below you. 1B—"

With wide excited eyes, the woman grabbed Dory's free arm and swung her into the apartment. "Oh! Yes dear! How lovely to meet you! Come in, come in."

Instantly, the scent of cat urine and sardines struck Dory. At first, she thought to react with disgust, yet quickly caught herself. She breathed through her mouth as she moved further inside. The apartment was filled to the brim with felines of all ages, sizes, and colors. They rested on furniture or hid under chairs, each of them staring at the guest with utter loathing. One striped tabby on a high shelf swiped her paw by Frank's nose with a hiss. The puppy snuggled against his mistress's side with a whimper.

"Bertram, behave yourself," the old woman cheerfully scolded. She turned to the couch, a ripped and abused piece of furniture covered in throw rugs to disguise the damage. Lifting a disdainful Persian and setting him on the floor, the woman stated, "Don't mind the babies. Oh my, little munchers! They think everything is theirs. Have a seat."

Dory settled on the very edge of the couch with Frank securely in her lap. The woman set herself on an overstuffed armchair that at one time had probably been white. Now it was a repulsive brown with faded patches of yellow. "Again, sorry to stop by like this I just wondering—" Dory started off but the woman waved her hands to interrupt.

"About the former tenant of your home? Of course, I'll fill you in." She continued before Dory could correct her. "The woman who lived there for the last fifty years was a bit of a hermit. She had no family, I never saw any friends come in. In fact, I rarely saw her leave the place. I didn't even know she had pets until after she passed on, poor old soul. Those three poor babies were hers."

The woman pointed her hand at a spot behind the couch. Dory twisted around and noticed three pathetic long haired cats wearing costumes. One was dressed as a little sailor in navy blue with a white hat held on by elastic. The second had been clothed in a blue raggedy doll dress covered in white polka dots. The third was the worst. His costume was a kitty replica of the Blue Boy painting, complete with frilly collar and four little black boots. Each looked more oppressed than the next with their little heads hanging under the weight of ridiculous hats.

The Crazy Cat Lady went on, pity thick in her tone, "She supported herself by making doll clothes, but apparently she made some kitty costumes too. I wish I'd known. I would have tried to rescue those three years ago. I don't approve of putting cats in clothes."

"Then why are they still wearing the costumes?" Dory asked curiously, watching the Raggedy Anne cat bat at her own yarn wig.

"The costumes are sewn on them and they're a tad gun-shy still," Crazy Cat Lady explained flippantly. "I can't get close enough to them to cut the silly things off. Probably comes from being alone in that apartment for so long. It was nearly a week before anyone realized that the poor soul in 1B had passed away."

Dory clutched Frank to her sharply. "She died there!"

Crazy Cat Lady blinked at Dory dumfounded. "Yes, dear. Didn't you know? Wasn't that explained when you took the apartment?"

Reaching for the lease folded in her pocket, but still keeping one arm tightly wrapped around Frank, Dory swatted away ideas of sinister deeds or murder mysteries. The little dog squirmed, anxious to chase one of the traumatized costumed cats. "Frank, no," she whispered in response to the dog's movement, and then turned back to her host. "I . . . that's what I wanted to ask about. There's a mistake in my lease and I don't know who I talk to about getting it fixed. I've never been in a situation before where they made me sign the lease through the e-mail. I've yet to talk to a single human being in-person. I don't know who can fix this."

"Oh, that would be the Landlord. He could fix it," the Crazy Cat Lady explained as a black and white feline gracefully curled up in her lap.

"Great! Is he across the hall?" Dory happily started to stand until the Crazy Cat Lady spoke again.

"Oh no, dear. He's on the tenth floor." The words were a little condescending, as if Dory had asked a time wasting question.

"Is that the top floor?" Dory wished to know, wondering how long it would take her to climb the stairs.

"Goodness gracious me, no. This building is seventeen floors tall! Wouldn't know it to look at it from the outside, would you." She sounded proud.

Dory didn't think the building looked tall enough to have the twelve floors she originally heard about. Then again, she been very busy staring at the ground when she moved in. "Can I just call the Landlord?" she asked, dreading the thought of trekking up nearly a dozen flights of steps.

"He doesn't have a phone. He keeps in contact through newsletters." The Crazy Cat Lady pulled a piece of paper out from under one of the cats, brushing the fur off of it carefully. "He's quite insightful. He puts these out to help us each with our problems."

Dory accepted the paper handed to her and read over the typed words. They were vague pieces of advice, reminding her of Sunday paper horoscopes or fortune cookie fates. She laid the paper atop a cat and sighed. "So I have to go all the way up there to talk to him."

The Crazy Cat Lady laughed a little as one of her darling pets bat at the newsletter, shredding it with fine tipped claws. "Of course. Just follow the staircases straight up. You can't miss his place. It fills the whole of the tenth floor and the door is painted the loveliest shade of green. He can sort out whatever mess you have with your contract. Just be sure not to go any higher than that."

"Why?" Dory asked, when in truth she thought, *"Why would I bother to explore this place?"*

"Because of your apartment's former owner's sister," the Crazy Cat Lady explained, not bothered by the mouthful of words.

"I thought you said you didn't know if she had any family?" Dory waved a hand distractedly in front of her face as wisps of fur floated in the sunlight rays.

"Oh, I didn't know until after the body was found. She is the most obnoxious neighbor who ever lived and she threw such a fuss when her older sister died. Apparently there was something in that apartment she wanted that wasn't with her sister's things. The Landlord wouldn't let her look for it. Now, there's a terrible fight going on between the two of them. If she finds out where you live, she'll be after you too." The woman's face creased with concern.

"Why won't the Landlord just let her have whatever it is?" Dory questioned aloud.

"The apartment was cleaned out. No one ever saw the object she was looking for," Crazy Cat Lady made clear with a little shrug. "At least not that I know of. I don't know why that obnoxious woman would want anything of her sister's. They weren't close and she never came down from the thirteenth floor to see her except, I've heard, for an odd Thanksgiving or two. They were both unnervingly unusual.

Promise me you'll steer clear of her."

"I promise," Dory said with ease having no intention in going near people who would hate her based on where she lived.

Standing and stuffing her lease back into her pocket, Dory felt the silver key slip out. As it fell to the ground, she leaned over to retrieve it and Frank escaped from her arms. The little dog terrorized through the apartment, barking and excitedly moving his stubby legs towards each kitten. He wagged his tail happily, expressing how it was playtime whether the cats knew this or not.

Chaos ensued and fur flew every which way as cats yowled. They scattered as Frank hopped into the air and back down in an attempt to keep up with their stylish movements. The Crazy Cat Lady waved her arms about and sprang from her seat. The cat in her lap tumbled to the floor and licked its paws indignantly.

"Oh my. Oh gracious!" the Crazy Cat Lady proclaimed over and over again.

Dory frantically called for Frank, but the dog was too caught up in joy to obey. At last, she gathered him into her arms once more just as the last of the cats jumped to a safe spot atop the counters and refrigerator of the tiny kitchen.

"Time for us to be going," Dory announced over the wrawls and hissing. "Thanks so much for the information. Sorry about Frank; he's just playful. Really sorry about this—" She paused to retrieve the silver key.

Much to her surprise the Crazy Cat Lady smiled. "Oh, I'm sure the little dears will be alright. They never get much excitement." She eyed the key in Dory's hand. "Where did you find that, dear?"

Glancing down at the key, she answered honestly, "In my apartment. I think it was left behind from years ago."

"Yes," the Cat Lady stated distractedly. Then, she kissed Dory on the forehead. The action seemed so random that Dory had no time to react or process before the Crazy Cat Lady added seriously, "You hold onto that key, dear. You never know when a key might come in handy." She exhaled loudly and gently led Dory out. "Off you go then."

Dory barely realized she was back in the hallway until the door shut behind her. She set down Frank and glanced down at him. The little dog was still panting from his adventure. "I can't take you anywhere, can I?" The dog wiggled at her merrily and they both started back down the stairs.

Chapter Three:
The Third Floor; How Dory Met the Ghost

Dory stopped back at her apartment to grab her jean jacket and changed from her sandals into her red high tops, muttering to Frank all the while. "I'm not about to walk all that away in these. I can't believe this. I have to climb ten floors just to get my lease fixed. This is ridiculous." She sighed, stopping her rant in order to think. "Complaining isn't going to help things, right?" Frank wagged his tail at her, wondering if he should answer. She looked down at him with her hands resting on her hips, "Ready to go?"

Frank tilted his head at her, not certain of what she was saying but thrilled that she was addressing him. Dory stuffed his leash into her pocket in case she'd need it and remembered to lock her apartment door behind them.

The upward bound staircase was dimly lit. The builders had obviously not had the insight to realize that most human beings needed light to travel steps. Dory tripped four times on her way up. By the fifth stumble, she landed face first on the landing of the third floor. Frank ran instantly to lick her face, taking advantage of her being at his level.

Dory felt a cool breeze pass over the wetness of her cheeks. Frank froze, the wiry hairs on his back standing on end. Moving into a sitting position, Dory realized she and the dog were alone in the eerie hallway. A broken light overhead flickered like a blinking eye creating shadows that moved across the floor towards her.

She scrambled to her feet, rubbing her hands over her arms to keep out the chill. Frank began to dance anxiously. "Stop that," she scolded. "You're freaking me out." The puppy replied with a whimper.

The cool breeze whipped passed the girl and her dog. The lights shot off. Frank's growls turned into barking. The lights flashed back to life as the dog's protests grew louder. A form manifested at the end of the hallway and Dory found herself unable to move.

It was a man, young and of an average build wearing jeans and an old navy blue tee shirt advertising some obscure band from the late sixties. The colors of his skin and clothes were washed out reminding Dory of trying to look out of her filthy bedroom window downstairs. His hair was a sandy color, sticking out every which way like straw. His hands and feet were larger than his frame, a little awkward in their design. His wide eyes were the lightest of blues, almost silver like. She could see right through him.

Dory's heart stopped in her chest as he watched. His round head tilted at the sight of her, taking a memory of her straight brown hair, rosy cheeks, and bright red sneakers. He took a single step towards her and Frank. The dog's barking halted in order to study the man with interest.

"Boo!" He lifted his arms over his head and waved his fingers as if he were doing choreography in an MGM musical.

Dory's body relaxed and she heaved a sigh. "Seriously?"

Frank yawned.

The ghost dropped his arms to his sides and sheepishly replied, "Um . . . yeah." His voice was not deep or imposing, just a voice not unlike the traffic reporter on her favorite radio station, the sort of voice that caught your attention, but was not interesting enough to be a regular D.J.

Critically, she told him, "No offense, but 'boo' was the best you could come up with? Haven't you ever seen a horror movie?"

Frank sat at the ghost's feet in order to support Dory's point.

The ghost shrugged. "I don't know. Give me a break. I don't have a TV. I hang out in a hallway."

"Why don't you go into the one of the apartments?" she asked motioning to lines of parallel doors.

He looked at her as if she had spoken a vile insult. "I'm a ghost, not a trespasser." His face scrunched into an embarrassed sneer. Besides, I can't always go completely through solid objects. I'm sorta a ghost in training, I guess." Defensive and upset, he hunched his shoulders and folded his arms in front of him.

"I don't believe in ghosts," she scoffed, yet kept her distance from the partially transparent man. Her own arms crossed over her chest and she tried not to think about how ludicrous she sounded to herself.

"You know, every time a person says that, a ghost somewhere falls down dead," he explained sadly, wagging his index finger at her.

Dory blinked once, processing this logic. "Aren't ghosts already dead?"

He smiled, losing his defensive stance and reveling in the conversation. "You're quick!" When Dory didn't smile back, his eyes fell and he rubbed the back of his neck. "Well, I guess I won't bother you anymore. I mean, I can't scare anyone else on this floor, what made me think I'd have better luck with someone who stumbled here." He settled himself on the upward steps and, downtrodden, held his head in his hands.

"I'm sorry," she told him feeling awful that she made a pathetic ghost feel inadequate. Dory sat down upon the step next to the partially transparent man. "Have you ever tried haunting on another floor? I saw three kids on my floor yesterday who look like they need to have the snot scared out of them."

The ghost sat a little taller. "Another floor? Huh. Never thought about that. Do you think I'm allowed?"

"Allowed? I don't know. What are the rules for haunted houses?" Dory noticed the ghost was slowly becoming less see-through. She wondered if he knew he was becoming solid or if it was automatic. Her eyes studied him intently. He was a science project.

"It probably depends on who makes up the rules for the house itself, I think. I mean, if there are other ghosts around, I don't want to get into a turf war or anything," he replied. "Who's in charge of this house?"

"The Landlord. I'm going to see him now about my lease because the Crazy Cat Lady said—" The moment after Dory spoke she regretted it. She could sense what was coming next and it did not please her.

"Hmm. And you should always listen to crazy cat ladies. Well great, I'll come with you!" the ghost exclaimed. He watched Dory's shoulders slump and he slipped back into transparency mode. "Unless . . . you don't want me to come with you."

Dory stared into the lost expression on his face, as well as the stair banister she could see on the other side of him. He held the slightest amount of hope, but that was not enough to keep him solid. Frank made a light whimper, as if also sensing the ghost's forlornness. Dory knew this was one of the reasons why she did not like getting to know her neighbors. She had trouble saying no to people in need. She also thought about being trapped in the basement during the storm. So many people in the same place, all frightened of the same thing, yet none of them would help one another.

"Oh, okay. Yes. I mean, yes. Sure, you can come with

me. Maybe we can find someone for you to scare on the way to the Landlord's office."

The ghost jumped energetically. "Awesome! Which way do we go?"

"Up," she told him as she motioned to the staircase she still sat on. At first, she estimated how much of the trip upstairs she could endure without establishing a permanent acquaintance with the dead guy, but she realized how eager he was to talk. Deciding to get formalities out of the way, she offered unwillingly, "By the way, I'm Dory. What's your name?"

The ghost opened his mouth to answer looking very confident in his knowledge as he stated, "Don't know."

Dory stood to face him. "You can't remember your name? What about anything about your life?"

"Nope. I think I remember dying though," he told her without reserve.

Thinking back on her own brief thoughts of death during the storm, she very quietly and carefully asked, "What was that like?"

"Cold. I think I fell someplace and when I landed it was cold," he told her with embarrassment. He added awkwardly, "I wish I had a better story to tell you."

Dory was not sure how to respond to him; he was the first dead person she had ever met. Clapping her hands together as a command, she quickly told him, "Well, if we're going to go, let's get going. Come on, Frank." The dog ran to her and waited for her to lift him. Dory stretched and sighed. She looked down at the spirit still perched on the steps. "I wish I had a name to call you. What about Casper?"

"How about we just stick to you calling me Ghost," he suggested. "It's easy to remember and I'll know to answer to it because I'm the only ghost here."

"What if we meet another ghost on the way?" Dory

challenged as she scooped Frank into her grip.

"Then you can call him Casper." Ghost hopped to attention and aimed his right hand up the stairs. "Off we go?"

Dory nodded at him, wondering if she should be more concerned that she was walking through the apartment building with a ghost, especially since she didn't believe in ghosts. All the same she let him walk first along the steps, leading the way to the fourth floor. "Better just not think about it," she said aloud.

"Not think about what?" Ghost asked with interest.

"Nothing. I was talking to myself." Dory realized she'd spent too much time talking to only Frank and tried to suppress the blush in her cheeks.

"Oh, I know all about that. I haven't had anyone to talk to for as long as I can remember. Most people just ignore me so I've had a lot of conversations with myself," he explained, his words tumbling out clumsily. "I'm sorry in advance if I say anything I shouldn't. I'm not really sure what I'm doing. It's hard to remember formalities when you don't remember being alive."

Dory was impressed with his honesty. For some reason, despite her annoyance at ghosts being real, she realized that she wanted to help him. The balloon of irritation welling within her chest vanished and she smiled the tiniest of smiles. "I'll let you know, but, really, you're doing fine."

"I'm a ghost who can't scare people," he countered. "I may not remember much, but plausibly that's not fine."

"You're like a misfit toy," Dory fussed sympathetically. "Maybe that's all you need, to remember what people are like and what scares them. Or a how about we find you a book like Haunting for the Inexperienced? Then you won't have to see the Landlord."

Ghost's expression turned skeptical, obviously

determined to continue with her on their journey.

Dory added, feeling like she was setting up the guy for failure, "I'm not really sure how the Landlord can help you with this."

"Maybe you're right—" Ghost tried to run his hand over the banister as they walked, but it went straight through. "But even if he can't help, I could always try to scare him when we get there."

"Do me a favor and try to scare him after I get my lease sorted out," she requested politely to hide her doubt in Ghost's scaring skills. She secretly hoped that when she died she was more competent than he.

Chapter Four:
The Fourth Floor; The Hallway Through the Fourth Floor

They approached the fourth floor landing and rounded a corner. The stairs ended at a wall at the edge of a corridor.

"What do we do now?" Ghost asked poking his transparent head into the wall as if to see if some steps were hidden there.

The young woman sighed heavily. The tapping of her foot echoed through the hall as she surveyed their surroundings. After a moment of contemplation, Dory pointed down to the end of the hallway. "The stairs must start again over there I think." As she went to investigate, she added with a grunt, "This place is a maze, I swear."

"Or a M.C. Escher painting," Ghost added, frowning at the trek they would have to make to the end of the hall.

Turning to him with surprise, Dory questioned, "You can't remember your life, but you know who Escher is?"

Ghost blinked several times, straining his mind against his own lack of knowledge. "Apparently," he concluded.

The stylized look of the building's interior had altered slightly. The entrances were plain with no design or flourish carved into the wood. The light fixtures which hung between the doors were the same geometric art deco design as the lamps hanging outside Dory's apartment, but the floor tiles and walls were a dull gray industrial. As they walked through the hallway, a door began to open. A young mom and her three scowling toddlers leaned out. Dory paused and Ghost turned invisible. Frank instantly ran towards one of the children excitedly. He sat down and held his front paws in the air, begging to be played with.

The mother of the child took out a broom and began to swat at Frank. "Shoo! Shoo now!" Her gaze locked upon Dory. "No solicitors!"

"I'm not selling anything," Dory said, holding up her arms in case the woman turned the broom on her. "I live downstairs. I'm just passing through."

"No! No! I don't want to buy anything! Thank you!" And with that the mom slammed the door.

At first, Dory stared at the shut barrier as if it had been the wood itself which had ranted at them. "Freeeaky," Dory sing-songed as she tiptoed passed the door.

"I agree," Ghost answered, his disembodied voice wafting by her like a comforting breeze. "And I know freaky."

"No, you don't," Dory giggled, not realizing how relaxed she had grown with her new colleague in just a matter of minutes.

Ghost reappeared and sighed, "No. No, I don't."

"Maybe if you didn't disappear you could actually scare someone," Dory pointed out, eying him disapprovingly.

"I'm not sure if anyone can see me when I'm visible. You're the first person to talk to me in a long, long time," Ghost told her. "Except for this one woman who always used to ask me to hold open the door for her when she had groceries. If I'd vanish, she would stand in the hallway and rant about the rudeness of all generations that weren't hers." Ghost thought back on the woman for another moment, then dropped one arm and motioned with his other hand to the rest of the hallway. "I'm starting to think this place really is weird."

Dory also pondered over the woman from his story and told Ghost, "No. People complaining is fairly normal." She tried to remember the number of times she had fought off solicitors at one of her previous apartments during her college years. A guy who sold insurance used to come by once a week until the entire building signed a restraining order against him.

Just then, a second door shot open. An elderly man leaning on a walker appeared. "I hear you out there, missy. I don't want to buy anything!" He snapped so loud that his teeth nearly leaped from his mouth.

Ghost stood very still, but the old man didn't seem to notice him. He was too busy shaking his wrinkled, arthritis ridden finger at Dory.

She insisted, "I'm not selling anything! I'm just—"

"I know every trick in the book, young woman, and I won't fall for it," he informed her harshly. "You and your see-through friend won't get me to buy any of your shoddy products or girl club cookies." He also slammed his door shut and turned the dead bolt with an earth shattering click.

"Now that . . ." Dory said as they walked passed the old man's door, "that was weird."

A third door opened and Dory groaned, "Oh for Pete's sake!"

This time, a sick man came out. He was in his thirties, dressed in sweat pants and a tee-shirt with a television corporation name stitched over the right breast. Frank growled at him and Dory realized it was the tactless fellow from earlier in the morning, his sickness having greatly paled his complexion in a short amount of time. Beads of sweat glistened in his blonde hair.

Ghost muttered to himself. "He needs zinc and vitamin C." Dory glanced at him from the corner of her eye yet Ghost did not seem to think anything of his random diagnosis.

The sick man held a Kleenex to his red nose and said through his stuffed, scratchy voice, "I'm not buying—"

"And I'm not selling!" Dory exclaimed. "I'm just walking through. Now, go back inside and please don't breathe on me."

"Heh," the man replied followed by a gravely hum echoing from within his chest. "Right. So you're just walking through? Then why are you dressed like someone who sells magazine subscriptions?"

Dory looked down at her top, jeans, and red Converse. "I do not." She then looked up and quietly asked with pain, "Do I?"

Seeing that she was obviously bothered by the comment, Ghost stepped up to the ill man. "Excuse me, but you just insulted my friend. Apologize."

The man sneezed, spraying snot and drool directly through Ghost. Dory ducked from the flying germs and said, "Don't worry about it, Ghost. Let's go."

The sick man then reached out a sweaty hand towards the top button of Dory's checkered top. "I remember you from earlier. You were . . . funny." The single word caused his lips to curl into a blinding smile. "You don't have to go. I might be persuaded to buy whatever you're selling if you're willing to stay for a little while and play nurse."

As his hand moved dangerously close to Dory's cleavage line, she swatted his fingers away and squeaked an appalled, "Eww."

"That's it!" Ghost snapped, stepping in front of Dory even though the man could still see her through the spirit. "He needs to say he's sorry. I don't care how sick his is; he shouldn't be such an ass."

"An ass? You're boyfriend isn't too bright, sweetie," the man observed. He broke into a violent coughing fit and wiped trickle of muck from the corner of his mouth.

"Apologize huh? Okay. Make me."

"Okay." Ghost determinedly inhaled. The hallway grew cold and the lights flickered. He faded in and out for a moment, mimicking the fluorescent overhead. He opened his mouth, his eyes glowing red, and he tried to use his deepest voice. "Apologize now! Or feel my wrath!"

Frank wagged his tail at the breathy sound of Ghost's threat as if someone had just told the dog is was dinner time. Dory winced at the sound, encompassing just how bad her new friend was at being a ghost.

The man was a little unnerved by the lights and breeze, hanging onto his door frame and glancing around like an excited bird. But when he heard Ghost's "scary" voice, he coughed out a laugh. "Nice try, buddy. What was that? Your best Darth Vader impression?" He turned to Dory, adding, "Hey, farm girl! Your friend looks sicker than me. You better get him home. Oh! And if you ever want to take up my nursing offer, I promise I'd make it worth your while."

"Drop dead." Dory bit back calmly.

The man shrugged, then continued to chuckle as he closed the apartment. Dory felt her breath quiver at the relief of the shut door.

Ghost's shoulders slumped. "He wasn't scared." The words were barely above a whisper. "And what was he talking about you playing nurse?" He thought about the way the sick man's fingers had reached out scandalously close to Dory's chest. "Oh, never mind," he amended, his semitransparent cheeks turning slightly pink.

Dory mulled over the moment, focusing her mine on Ghost's predicament. A haunt who could not haunt really was a dismal sight. "It's alright that he wasn't scared. We'll work on it. The red eyes thing was good."

"Yeah?" He turned hopeful.

"Yeah." She smiled. "I'm sure we will find plenty more

people for you to practice on. If everyone's going to be jumping out to accuse us of soliciting you'll get lots of chances."

"What about the voice?" His tone was still full of aspiration.

"We can work on the voice," she told him truthfully. "How long have you actually been dead? Why haven't you been practicing?"

"I have. I'm just not entirely sure what I'm supposed to be doing," Ghost clarified.

"What's that like, not having anything to refer to?" Dory observed him, trying to think of people in her own life she could compare him to, grasping at clues to who he might have once been. She told him plainly, "You can talk just fine and you're smart, I can tell that."

"You think I'm smart?" he asked with surprise.

`"Well, you certainly aren't an idiot. You're just sort of . . . naive, not that that's a bad thing," Dory stated quickly, trying as hard as she could not to insult the spirit. "He saw you. I guess people on the other floor just ignore you. How do you control the lights like that?"

"Oh that. I can mess with anything electrical. I just tap into the energy it gives off and take it from there." He pointed upward to a sconce on the wall and the light bulb within began to blink uncontrollably. "It keeps me entertained."

"I think it's brilliant. You should use more of that." She pointed to the end of the hallway. Frank trotted alongside her, glancing at each door to check for more people. "We're almost there. I can see the staircase from here."

"And no more doors are opening. I think we're in the clear." Ghost added, "Hey if we do run into another ghost, can we have him or her tag along so I can pick their brain?"

"I don't see why not. As long you two don't electrocute me or burn down the building. Where's my dog?" Frank had stalled a foot behind them, his little nose wiggling uncontrollably. Dory looked down at Frank. "What's with you?" Then she smelled it.

Chapter Five:
The Fourth Floor: The Rescue of Raleigh

The hallway was growing warm and Frank stood perfectly still at the apartment door closest to the stairs. He whined a little as he waited for his mistress and the ghost to catch up.

Dory smelled the still, heavy air. "What's that?"

"What's what?" Ghost asked, spinning around in a brave, prepared for anything stance.

"Do you smell smoke?" she asked worriedly.

"I don't smell anything," Ghost pointed out. "My senses really don't work that well. I am dead, you know."

They took a couple more steps along the hall. The scent burned against Dory's nostrils and Frank began to sneeze, rubbing at his nose with his paw. "Something is definitely burning. Why don't you poke your head into some of these apartments and find out where it's coming from?"

"I already told you, I don't like doing that," he said. "How would you like it if a ghost was always spying on you and you never knew it?"

"Someone could be in trouble. I doubt they're going to care about their privacy if their whole apartment is going to burn down," Dory insisted. "I think the smell is coming from one of these."

Dory pointed to three doors lining the left side of the hallway, opposite from the upward staircase. Suddenly, yelling emanated from one of the three homes. At first it was a surprised gasp of pain. Quickly, it turned to an agonized scream. "I'm sure you at least heard that," she said to Ghost with annoyance.

The Ghost was already at the door, poking his head through the wood and coming back out with a horrific expression. "There's a man on fire. What do we do?"

Dory rammed her shoulder against the barrier, but her thin frame did little damage. She tried again. The locked snapped hard against itself and the door barely moved.

Ghost waved his hands in a panic. "Fire thing—"

"Yes, Ghost, man is on fire! If you can't help then please don't state the obvious," Dory responded as she repeatedly ran herself into the wood and shouted for help from anyone who might be in one of the other apartments. She glanced up at the ceiling. "Why aren't the smoke alarms going off? This place is so not up to code!"

Ghost began to hop up and down. "No, the fire thing— The extinguisher! By the staircase! You can use it to break the door down, can't you?"

Dory made a dash for the fire extinguisher hanging on the wall. It was locked into its glass case. Flinging off her jacket, she wrapped the denim around her hand and punched through the glass. A shard bit into her knuckle. Her brain did not pause to register the gash in her flesh. Instead, she took the red metal cylinder in both hands and crashed it down upon the door handle of the burning man's flat. Beating and hammering at the handle, at last it came off and landed at her feet.

She and Ghost rushed in. Shadows and patches of pitch blackness hugged the room, all for a single strip of light from a window giving a warm glow to the sparse furniture. A figure lay on the floor, writhing in pain. His skin smoked and short flame spurts burst from every inch of him. Dory hesitated, wondering if the extinguisher foam would work on a human.

"Get a blanket," Ghost ordered, his hands ringing and itching to be of use. "We need to smother the flames."

Dropping the red metal cylinder, she ran to the closest piece of furniture and pulled blanket out from amongst the other bedding. She laid it across the man, tossing it from a safe distance, and started commanding him to roll. When the flames died down, the young woman dropped to his side, gently patting him down. Warmth lightly toasted her fingers through the fabric. She breathed outward to avoid the sickening smell of baked flesh.

Ghost tried to inspect the victim. "Careful with the blanket. If the burns are really bad the fabric might pull off his skin. Call the hospital. They can treat burns better than we ever could."

She could feel the heat through the blanket subsiding. The man's breathing was heavy from under the cover, but his screams stopped as he rolled back and forth while Dory continued to reach lightly across the comforter. Dory barely heard his muffled shout. "Kuvvrrrrthawendo".

"What did he say?" Ghost asked, feeling worthless as he hovered over Dory and the burning man.

Dory glance around the flat. Every window except one was boarded up so tightly that no light could get in. Like a fallen soldier, a plank lay below the single window providing sunlight. "I think he said cover the window," she replied.

Ghost pointed at the phone hanging in the kitchen. "If I was him I'd want an ambulance called first."

She rose from the floor beside the burn victim. "Maybe he's light sensitive," she suggested and took the fallen board from the floor. Nails stuck out of it from either end which she pushed back into place amongst the other pieces of lumber against the window. They were left in utter darkness, but Dory still called out, "It's covered. Do you want us to call the hospital now?"

The man sat upright, his blanket falling down from his face. He didn't have a burn or a single sign of scorched skin. Hairline trails of smoke still rose from his clothing, which was tattered and black from the fire. He looked directly at Dory and smiled. "Won't be necessary. I'm quite better now. Lousy carpentry. Next time I'll splurge and get the sheet metal to go over it. Or bricks. I think bricks would fit into that window sill nicely."

He got up from the floor and crossed the room. He switched on the light and a cheap lamp in a corner came on. The first thing to catch Dory's attention was the item of furniture she had taken the blanket from. It was a coffin, sitting open at the center of the room. Beyond the refrigerator, lamp, and a chest of drawers, the coffin was the only furnishing on display. Dory jumped to her feet and started gradually for the unlocked front door.

"Glad to see you're okay. Well, my dog's waiting for me . . ." She waved at Ghost to follow, uncertain if the coffin sleeper could see him or not.

The grinning burn victim slapped his hands over his arms and ash clouded over him like a comic book character in need of a bath. "Oh no! This shirt's ruined. Wait just a minute and I'll change." The man zipped over to the drawers, retrieving a new shirt and pants, then into a door that Dory assumed lead to a bathroom.

As the bathroom light clicked on and they heard the rustle of fabric, Dory turned to Ghost. "We need to leave."

"He has a coffin," Ghost stated, pointing at the unusual central piece of the living room. "Do you think he got that at one of those Swedish furniture stores?"

"No, I don't. I think it's time to go," she whispered. Her heart had sped up and her palms produced a thin layer of sweat.

Just as she turned, the bathroom door opened again. Their host was well built with a toned body and lean face.

His cheek bones created perfect symmetrical lines leading down to his strong chin. He wore a gray button up shirt over a pair of dark gray slacks. His shoes looked expensive like Italian leather. His hair, despite the previous burning, was a dark auburn color combed back skillfully as if an artist had painted it there. His skin was pale and his lips were a little thin, but this made his eyes stand out with an amazing blue brilliance.

"Thanks for the rescue," he expressed. "Like you said, I have a light sensitivity problem."

"That why you have a coffin?" Ghost asked as Dory edged toward the door.

"Oh that! Halloween decoration that I can't find any place to store. I just keep it out. Makes for a good conversation piece." The man waved his hand as the coffin flippantly, trying to suppress a grin.

The front door had been left open a crack and Frank nudged until it allowed for just enough room which he could squeeze in. The little dog wandered in like he owned the apartment.

Dory moved towards the dog to pick him up when Ghost exclaimed, "Blood!"

"What?" she practically screamed checking the floor and the translucent man.

Ghost rushed over to her and tried to lift up her hand. Instead, she felt a chill move through her arm as his hand went directly through her skin. She shivered, but Ghost continued without noticing. "There," he said, discouraged that he could not help her.

Dory glanced down at the blood seeping through the gash in her hand. "That must have happened when I broke the fire extinguisher case. Why was it even locked?"

"Because this place is weird," Ghost replied, and then noticed the unusual expression on their new acquaintance's face. The man's blue eyes were focused intently on Dory's hand. He ran his tongue over his bottom lip and released a heaving breath. A small amount of drool trickled from the corner of his mouth. "What's with you?" Ghost asked the man.

Just then the man lunged at Dory's hand, his mouth wide open. Fangs protruded from his upper gum. Dory let out a scream and backed away. Ghost tried to come between them, but the man just ran straight through him.

At that time, he stopped, as if to gasp for air. He ran to his refrigerator and took out a clear plastic packet with something dark red swishing back and forth within. He sank his teeth into the plastic and began to drink greedily. When the plastic bag was empty and deflated, he breathed a sigh of relief then tossed it into the sink.

"Sorry about that, sweetness," he said casually as he sauntered back towards them.

Ghost set himself in front of Dory, despite the fact that it wouldn't do any good as protection. She stuffed her bleeding hand into her jeans pocket and stated, "A vampire."

"Fraid so, my love," he told her with a suave smile. "I'm Raleigh Hemphill."

"I'm not your love," she countered with a certain amount of bitterness.

"Well . . . if you tell me your name I won't call you that anymore." He was confident, standing with ease as if it were perfectly normal to be a vampire introducing himself to a woman that could be his future meal.

"Don't tell him," Ghost pleaded.

Watching the vampire carefully, she at last said, "Dory."

"Why did you tell him? He just tried to bite you!" Ghost asked in a squeaky voice, nearly having a heart attack (or the dead person equivalent to one).

"If he's going to kill me and eat me, I'd rather I go with

my real name being used not some disgusting derogatory pet name," Dory proclaimed.

"Oh, good God, a woman's advocate," Raleigh teased then looked at Ghost with compassion. "Do you put up with this all the time?"

Her back straightened a little and Dory addressed the vampire again. "So, Raleigh, what happens now?"

"Brave." With an impressed smirk, he jerked his head towards the kitchen sink. "There are some paper towels in the cupboard. First thing is first, I'm going to go sit in my coffin and rest while you run your hand under the tap. Stop it from b-b-b-b-b— from bleeding so I won't be tempted." Even the word blood seemed to make him a little anxious.

Ghost leered at the vampire's plan. "Can we trust you to stay in your coffin while she cleans up?"

Raleigh countered with, "Can I trust you two to not shut the lid on me, douse it in gasoline, and burn me alive? Or rather undead, as the case may be."

Dory stepped between the two men, her hand still securely in her pocket. "It's a deal. But if you make a move towards me again with those fangs, I pull the boards off the windows."

Holding up his hand in mock surrender, Raleigh pushed out his bottom jaw and muttered, "That's only fair."

As she moved into the kitchen and the vampire went to sit upright in his morbid bed, Dory asked, "This catching on fire thing, does it happen to you often?"

"Oh, you mean almost being burnt like a crispy critter in my own apartment? It's happening more and more lately. Whoever boarded up these windows did a shoddy job of it. I really ought to complain to the Landlord."

"Oh." This time Dory kept her mouth shut about where she was headed. She glanced at Ghost to do the same, but it was obvious the spirit had no intention of inviting the creature of the night along with them.

"So, Miss Dory . . . or is it Ms. these days? Either way, what are you and the spook up to?" Raleigh asked as he settled back comfortably against the red cushions of his coffin. Dory had to admit, despite the gruesome idea of sleeping in a box intended for the dead and having a lid shut on you, the interior of his coffin did look comfortable. Every muscle of the vampire relaxed as he melted into the sheets. It made her think of a long sofa stuffed into a container so all of the pillows were bunched into a thick padding.

Turning on the water and focusing on the crimson escaping from her wound, Dory simply said, "Ghost and I are new friends." Her breath caught in her throat as she felt the sting of the warm liquid on the cut. Ghost hovered nearby, supervising the cleaning as if it was something he had done a million times.

"Oh, I see," Raleigh replied. He stayed flat in his coffin, but one arm rose up to shake a finger in Ghost's direction, "You been spying on the young lady, you cad?"

Instantly insulted by the remark, Ghost spat back, "You're one to talk! You just tried to—"

"Ghost, settle down. I'm alright. You're alright. Frank is alright. No harm done. Let's just get my hand clean and we can go," she said more to the vampire than to the ghost.

"Frank?" Raleigh asked, sitting up slightly. At the sound of his name, the dog sat forward and wagged his tail. "Oh," the vampire responded with disappointment, "the mutt."

"He is not a mutt!" Dory snapped, shaking her wet hands about and spraying water over the vampire's kitchen.

"Who needs to calm down now?" the vampire chuckled. "He's just a dog, for crying out loud."

Dory gathered up a handful of paper towels and pressed them against her knuckle. "He might be just a dog to you, but to me . . . he's my dog, so shut up."

Raleigh perched upright completely with a loud huff. "Being a little sensitive, aren't you?"

"Being a little bit of an ass, aren't you," Dory countered, then paused to make certain the cut had stopped bleeding. The red around the edges had turned brown and she hoped the wound would scab over quickly.

"What are you doing?" Ghost panicked. "Why are you making the guy with the sharp pointy fangs mad at you?"

Like a child, Dory extended her finger at the vampire and pouted, "He started it."

The vampire chuckled and climbed back out of his coffin. Instantly, Ghost was at Dory's side again even though Raleigh was not advancing in her direction. He rubbed the back of his neck and said, "I suppose I did start it. You'll have to excuse me. One of the disadvantages to being a vampire is you look human. You walk and talk and do laundry, but lose something too."

"The ability to digest actual food?" Ghost guessed, half inquisitively.

"That and basic human empathy. You can still think human, there's even a form of love amongst vampires. But it's not the same. I miss . . ." He looked whimsical for a long moment. "What am I telling this to you two for? Weren't you leaving?"

Much to her own surprise, Dory moved a little closer to him and gently pried, "What do you miss?"

Raleigh half laughed but it was humorless noise full of self-pity. "I can't believe I'm about to say this out loud. The vampire who sired me would be tossing her blood if she heard me but . . . Okay; you have to promise not to tell."

"Who are we going to tell?" Ghost pointed out. "She talks to her dog all day and I'm dead."

"I don't talk to my dog all day," Dory justified.

"I miss having a heart."

"Right! To munch on!" Ghost spat.

Raleigh went on without insult. "I miss feeling real feelings, real compassion . . . real love."

"Aren't vampires supposed to be the seducers and conveyers of love," Dory guessed. Raleigh's deep blue eyes avoided her clinical expression. "Or is that a myth."

"No. Seduction is supposed to be how we, um . . . catch our food," Raleigh explained with slight embarrassment. "But that's not really the kind of love I mean. I don't even mean a romantic love. I'm talking about basic human kindness and—"

"And sensitivity? The same thing you were just criticizing me for," Dory clarified with a low whistle.

"You see my problem," Raleigh said with a small amount of apology in his voice.

"But won't having empathy and caring get in the way of your, eh, diet?" Ghost asked, glancing back at the fridge with disgust.

Raleigh opened his fridge to show off the assortment of plastic plasma bags all stacked upon the shelves. He waved a hand at his supply, the light from the fridge catching on the single ruby ring he wore. "My diet is based around blood banks and large livestock like cows and sheep. I have not drunk blood directly from a human in nearly ten years. I'm in a support group. They'll be disappointed in me when I tell them about today." He looked mournfully at Dory's hand. "Sorry about that, I just haven't smelled blood fresh from a human in a while. I got the shakes."

He turned, closing the fridge and pointing at the boarded up windows. "I should point out I was in a weakened condition thanks to whatever carpenter did that job. I've tried to fix them myself, but it never works." He stuffed his hands into his pockets and relaxed his shoulders, smiling at the pair of them. "I think I've given you both enough excitement for one day. I'll let you get going. If you think of it, stop by again. I promise I won't try to bite anyone."

As he started to move to the door, he paused to pat Frank on the back as if silently expressing regret for calling the dog a mutt. Ghost leaned down and whispered to Dory, "Maybe we should take him with us."

Dory's surprise expression gaped at him, "Really? What happened to you being all protective and stuff?"

With a shrug, Ghost went on, "He needs help, in more ways than one. We can't help him with the whole feelings thing, but I bet the Landlord could at least fix his windows. And if he tries anything we can always toss him outside into the daylight."

"I had to pick up a thoughtful ghost, didn't I," Dory grumbled. He wiggled his eyebrows at her pleadingly. "Okay, fine. But if he kills me and drinks my blood, I'm haunting your dead butt to the end of eternity."

"Oh good. Company." Dory gave Ghost a horrified look. "I was kidding," he added quickly.

Dory walked over to Raleigh decidedly. "Here's the thing. We're going to see the Landlord about my lease and about where he's allowed to haunt. Do you want to come with us and ask about your windows? But no biting."

"Really?" He kicked his leather shoe along a scuff on the floor timidly, then, as if he'd forgotten himself momentarily, he straightened up and answered, "Sure! Why not? You two could probably use someone to look out for you in this place, anyway. Let me pack a cooler, just in case I get hungry."

He went back to the kitchen and retrieved a red and white container from a cupboard as well as an ice pack from the freezer. He piled three bags of blood in on top of the frozen block of liquid and plastic then closed up the cooler. He swung it alongside of him as he walked over to the waiting pair, like a child with a lunch pail.

"Off we go then?" he asked.

Dory looked at the cooler, a little sickened, but swallowed her disgust and answered, "Yep. Let's get this over with."

Ghost also watched the cooler with interest. "We're only going up a few flights of stairs. Why do you need a cooler?"

"You must both be new here." Raleigh chuckled, taking out his apartment key from his pocket. "You obviously don't know very much about this building." He frowned at the broken handle and reluctantly put his key away once again.

"Besides the fact that it gets freakier by the minute, no I don't know very much," Dory admitted as she collected Frank in order to carry him up the next staircase. Hugging the dog to her, Dory hoped the vampire could not see the fear that gripped her at his words. She waited on the first step. "Do I really want to know anything else?"

Raleigh waved his hand along the hall, motioning to the two rows of closed doors. "The Landlord is famous for renting to the . . . non-human variety of being."

"Meaning vampires?" Dory sounded skeptical.

Raleigh nodded, pursing his lips. "That's an example. But there are other things, dark things. Not sure why he does it. I've never actually met the man myself. I once heard from one of the other tenants that he was collecting supernatural creatures to protect himself from an evil wizard whose powers he'd stolen."

"Was Bilbo Baggins there?" Dory sarcastically remarked, "Or maybe the White Witch of Narnia?"

"This isn't a joke. It's very dangerous to go through this building beyond the third floor. You'll never know what you'll find." Raleigh placed a hand on Dory's arm, tapping her elbow like he was trying to grab her attention. "Now that I've told you this, you might not want to go on."

Ghost hovered at the bottom stair. "Just out of curiosity and not because I'm scared, are any of these immortal whatever's able to hurt a ghost?"

Raleigh spoke with truth in his tone, "I've heard there are creatures who feed off a person's energy or soul. Hate to break it you, pal, but you're nothing but energy."

"I'm not nothing but—"

"That's all a ghost is," Raleigh corrected. "You're a memory."

With a sigh, Ghost decidedly agreed, "That does make sense. I don't have a body and I'm not really here or there. I suppose I don't really have much to be scared of when I'm not really here." He glanced at Dory. "But maybe we better go back. This place can't be very safe for humans."

"Oh, for Pete's sake!" Dory started up the stairs, setting down her dog so her hands were free to wave around and illustrate her rant. Annoyance overtook her fear as she remembered the incorrect document burning a hole in her jeans pocket. "I'm not going to be afraid of some rumors. Besides, you're a ghost, you can go invisible and check ahead for danger. And you're a vampire. I'm sure you're tougher than most other things in this place. I, for one, am going to see the Landlord and get my lease fixed. Come on, Frank." The little dog ran after her as she ascended to the next floor. She paused at the top of the stairs, looking back at the two with a smirk. "Are you guys still with me?"

The ghost and vampire shrugged at one another then followed the young woman up to the fifth floor.

Chapter Six:
  The Fifth Floor; The Agoraphobic Werewolf

Just like the fourth floor, the fifth floor had split the staircases between both ends of the gray corridor. The group continued their conversation as they walked, each one wondering what could be lurking behind the many doors. No sounds came from behind the wood panels, making the three feel very alone as they moved hesitantly across the dirty corridor.

"Well, if the Landlord rents to supernatural beings, maybe you have an apartment here, Ghost, and you just don't remember," Dory suggested.

At first Ghost looked hopeful, but Raleigh was quick to crush this idea. "The Landlord would never lease to a ghost; they can't pay rent."

With a slight pout, Ghost answered, "I feel discriminated against."

"I feel discriminated against for you," Dory agreed. "We can complain about that when we see the Landlord too."

Raleigh eyed the two with a weary expression. "You really think you can just go around demanding things of a man that might have dark powers? I mean, I'm a—What do they call us in the movies? A 'creature of the night' and I wouldn't mess with this guy."

"Creatures of the night are what Dracula called the wolves not what people called him," Dory corrected. "Don't you know your own culture?"

"Give me a break. Bela Lugosi is not my culture. The man looked good in a cape and had a great accent, but he does not represent my people." Raleigh paused and added, "However, I'd prefer him as a mascot over Gary Oldman's Dracula. He was an awfully whiny son of a gun."

"He had emotion," Dory pointed out, "The exact thing you're complaining that you don't have. If you don't want to be whiny then don't try empathy."

Ghost broke into Dory's scolding with, "I think I know what you're both talking about. Was the Bela Lugosi movie the one where he was the gypsy and he turns into a wolf at night? Then he bites that other guy who then turns into a wolf too?"

"That was Wolf Man," Dory corrected, then softly coaxed. "Dracula is different. Remember anything about Dracula? It was about a vampire."

Ghost thought long and hard, picking at his few fragments of memories. "Was there a man who ate flies?"

"That's the movie!" Dory told him excitedly. "See, you can remember stuff."

"Yeah, some things I can," Ghost clarified. "I liked the guy who ate flies. He was funny." Ghost cleared his throat and began to rant in a raspy voice, "Flies! Flies! Who wants to eat flies? Give me a spider!"

Dory giggled. "That's pretty good. Maybe you should try that to scare people."

"Can we change the subject?" Raleigh asked, "This is my heritage you two are mocking."

"Oh, look who's sensitive about something," Dory teased. "We'll stop, but only because you're showing a whiny emotion, we are going to continue to talk about Wolf Man. I want to see how much Ghost can remember."

"What do I care if you talk about werewolves? Slobbering, clumsy beasts that serve no higher purpose other than fertilizing park trees and keeping the squirrel population down," Raleigh gruffly replied.

"And what higher purpose do vampires provide?" Ghost wanted to know, giving Dory a little wink as she laughed.

Raleigh proudly answered, "Hey! Vampires have done more in helping cure blood diseases than another race on the face of the earth!"

"But for purely selfish reasons," Dory added. She stopped and looked down at her little dog. "Besides, Frank loves werewolf movies. Every time one of them howls on the TV, he howls along. It's hilarious."

"You are way too obsessed with that dog," Raleigh grumbled.

Frank gave the vampire a dirty look as if he understood what they were saying, then ran ahead down the hallway. "I think you insulted him again," Ghost said as the little dog paced along the middle of the hallway, waiting for them to catch up.

Dory defended her puppy. "And it really is funny the way he howls. He's so young he doesn't really have a howl yet. I sound more like—"

Just then, a yipping sound followed by a long, high pitched bellow echoed down the fifth floor hallway. Frank had his head tilted back and his lips barely parted as he tried to howl. He danced outside one of the doors in the hallway, scratching at the crack underneath and desperately wanting to go inside.

"Like that," Dory finished with confusion. She ran over to her little pet and knelt beside him. Setting a hand on his furry back, she asked, "What's with you? What are you howling at?"

"He's going to attract the attention," Raleigh hissed as he also crouched over Frank who was once again struggling to dig into the floor under the door.

"Good. Someone to try scaring," Ghost responded

with a wicked gleam in his eye.

"Uh, no. Bad," Raleigh replied. "Someone to scream, attract more neighbors and get us in big trouble. Were you two not listening when I said the whole other monsters living here thing? We do not need a House of Frankenstein moment."

"Conversation comes full circle," Dory muttered to herself, then tried to lift Frank into her arms. The puppy scrambled free and pressed himself against the apartment door. His tail wagged and his front feet pawed at the wood. "There must me another dog in there," Dory explained. "He always acts like this when he wants another dog to play with him. Completely tore up one of my aunt's flower beds in an attempt to play with her Frison Brise once."

"People still have flower beds?" Ghost asked. "I remember flower beds. I think I hate peonies."

"Didn't you bring a muzzle for him and something to shut up the dog too," Raleigh suggested as he tried to grab Frank, but the dog continually jumped out of reach then ran back to the door.

"I don't muzzle my dog!" Dory stated with horror. "He's just a puppy. He's learning."

"A puppy that might get us all destroyed if the wrong thing hears him," Raleigh argued harshly.

"Yelling isn't going to solve anything," she snapped back, then turned back to Frank, "Frank, that's enough. Settle down."

The little dog whimpered and sat, but would not budge from the door. Dory stood up and set her hands on her hips. "There. He's quiet. Happy?"

Raleigh also stood at full height, but before he could answer, the apartment door flew open. A pair of hands grabbed Frank, pulled him inside, and shut the door again before any of them could react.

Dory instantly ran at the door, pounding her fists

against the wood. Ghost passed directly through her and the door, following Frank into a dark home. It wasn't nearly the stumbling darkness that Raleigh's home had been, but shadows veiled each corner. The curtains were an ugly brown and the family room furniture had been covered in plastic. Large tubs, each one labeled with a typed sticker, lined the wall just below the windows. At the opposite side of the apartment was a kitchen with heavy blades hanging from a utensil organizer and the corner of bloody butcher paper hanging over the top of the trash can.

Ghost could hear Frank's barks coming from the bedroom at the back of the apartment. He ran at the noise and was met with the sight of the little dog sitting atop a pile of torn up bedding and a man, covered in hair from his face to the back of his hands, trying to chain himself to a wall. The bedroom was sparse, full of overturned chairs and devoid of pictures on the walls. The chains seemed to be the closest thing to décor.

Fur peaked out from under than man's collar, seeming to grow longer as Ghost watched. Frank's yips grew more frantic. The man was full of pain as he muttered to himself, "Too late! Too late!" His face contorted and he screamed in anguish. Ghost could hear bones breaking and reassembling inside the man's body like dry wood being cracked. Between his tortured yells, the man would order Frank, "Shut up! Shut up! I should have thrown you out the window! Ahhh!"

He doubled over, his hands still shackled to the blank wall of his bedroom. The sides of his face extended and his ears slid up to the top of his head before pointing upward in a triangle shape. His nose, fur covered and flat, began to extend from his face. His bottom jaw stretched out to follow until he grew a snout. His hairy hands remained hands, with five digits spreading out in agony, but his nails ripped through his skin. They became five claws which caught the wallpaper and matched dozens of other similar marks below the shackles he had obviously left behind before.

Ghost backed away, waving at Frank to follow him. "Uh . . . Mr. Wolfman. If you keep doing that to the wall you'll never get back your deposit."

The werewolf snarled in response, lunging at Ghost. The chains kept him a safe distance away, but it was obvious that all parts of the screaming man had faded into the growling monster who drooled as he gnashed his fangs.

The front door of the apartment still resounded with Dory's pounding which was now added to by Raleigh's shouts. At last, they managed to jimmy the lock open and run into the well-kept living room. Frank ran into Dory's awaiting arms and Ghost met them with a panicked expression.

"Time to go! Dory, you first. Let's keep moving."

"What is that?" Dory asked trying to see through Ghost and into the bedroom.

"A werewolf," Raleigh said with awe. "I knew they existed, but I never thought I'd meet one. They usually live in the country. They're just as disgusting as I thought."

Dory scowled. "I don't care what he is." She handed Frank off to Raleigh who held the dog out in front of him like a dirty rag. Marching into the bedroom without any fear in her posture, Dory turned to the snarling beast.

"I wouldn't do that," Ghost warned while Raleigh watched in stunned silence. The creature strained against his bindings, sniffing violently at the young woman as she came near.

Dory faced the brute and slapped him sharply on the nose. Ghost and Raleigh hung in the doorway as the confused werewolf transformed back into a man.

The bewildered man remained chained to the wall wrinkling his human nose as Dory started to shout. "What are you doing stealing people's dogs?!"

"You hit me," was all he managed to say in a withered voice, tears hanging on the edge of his words. "Why did you do that? Do you know how many germs are on the human hand? I might get sick now."

Dory was in no way swayed by his whining. "Oh, I'll give you something to be sick about! Why did you steal my dog? What did he ever do to you?"

Breathing heavily like he would sob at any minute, the man murmured, "I was trying to . . . to keep him quiet. I didn't want to change."

"Excuse me?" Dory scoffed. "You're blaming a puppy for your . . . condition."

"Dogs can trigger it," he meekly explained, his hands limply hanging by the wrists from the chains.

"Then you could have asked me to keep him quiet," Dory told him calmly, attempting to hold back the apology beginning to creep into her tone.

His hands dropped limply again then swayed a little against his shackles. He muttered something and hung his head so it mimicked his hands.

"What did you say?" Dory asked, her voice harsher than the rebuking anger that was still on her surface.

"I said," he repeated, his voice still just above a whisper, "I was scared."

Dory took a good long look at the man. His skin was a dusty color and his clothes, a yellow polo shirt and a pair of khakis, reminded her of a yuppie at a tennis match despite the rips from his transformation. He was tall, at least six foot three, with broad shoulders and a square head. His timid attitude seemed the complete opposite of his football player build. "You're afraid of people? A big guy like you?" she said with disbelief.

"I don't want to hurt people," he confessed. He eyed the two men still hovering in the doorway. "And . . . well, people make me nervous." As he spoke, the wall connected to his shackles gave way. The chains came off and the plaster-a-Paris fell down around the man's shoulders. He wailed, "I needed those!"

"Well, you should have known that would happen eventually," Ghost pointed out. "Dry wall really shouldn't support those heavy chains."

The werewolf pulled up his shackles like gaudy bracelets. "What am I going to do now? These chains were working so well."

With a sigh, Dory turned to Frank, Raleigh, and Ghost. Knowing what she was silently telling them, Ghost shrugged while Raleigh shook his head back and forth emphatically. Frank just wagged his tail. She looked at the werewolf who mournfully removed his chains as if saying goodbye to an old friend. "What's your name?"

"Winston," he told her as he pushed away the chains with a dejected expression.

"I'm Dory. This is Raleigh and . . . we just call him Ghost. And the puppy is Frank." She released another long exhale, wondering if she would regret her third invitation of the day. "We're going to see the Landlord about our own problems. Do you want to come with us and see if he can install something else in here to keep you . . . restrained?"

Winston straightened his back and his left eye twitched. "You want me to leave the apartment?"

"She doesn't want you to do anything," Raleigh corrected. "She's just trying to help you." He groaned and muttered to Ghost, "Werewolves. Stupid werewolves."

The werewolf shook and stood, his arms crossed over his chest insecurely. "I—I—I don't leave the apartment. It's been y—years. Ever since I was bit—"

"You mean you purposely shut yourself in . . ." Raleigh paused to look around the meager possessions each placed in a specific spot around the flat and spoke the last word of this sentence with disapproval, "here?"

"I like it," Winston said in a garbled voice as he tried to clean up the mess of drywall and torn wallpaper. "It's my home."

"But if you can't feel safe here," Dory offered, "is it really your home?"

Winston seemed to mull over her words while he cleaned. Despite his guests, he continued to brush the bits of wall into his hand, then walk over to a trash bin to discard them. The entire time, Raleigh complained, begging to just leave the werewolf behind. Dory said nothing. She watched patiently as he tidied up.

When he was finished the only evidence of the collateral damage that remained was the open hole showing the pipes and electrical wires in the wall. He adjusted his polo shirt and told Dory, "Just let me put on some shoes." He went to his closet, but paused to watch Raleigh pass Frank to Dory. "Is the animal coming?"

"We'll try to keep him at a safe distance from you," Dory offered.

"And if you turn into a wolf, I can restrain you," Raleigh boasted. "I do have a certain amount of strength of my own." Winston opened his mouth to argue, but Raleigh cut him off. "I'm a vampire. My species has always done pretty well at holding off your species."

"Oh." Winston, obviously terrified of Raleigh, edged around the corners of his room and waited for the vampire to move before passing though the doorway out to the family room.

Ghost waved his translucent hand in front of his own face. "And if you turn wolf I can walk through walls. I'm not sure how that helps, but I can do it."

"This is nuts," Raleigh stated.

Dory smiled at Ghost for his efforts and then turned to the other two companions. Already, she pondered how she would be able to babysit the three of them and felt a pain of regret at her decision to invite them all. *"Too late now,"* she thought, remembering to keep the words in her mind. She shouldered her way by them and out of the apartment. Out loud, she announced, "Everyone ready? Let's get this over with."

Chapter Seven:
  The Sixth Floor; The Journey to the Landlord

The odd group moved up to the following floor. The hall was darker than the past five floors. A couple of the light bulbs had burnt out within several sconces. The paint on the wall had faded and grime caked the bottoms of their shoes.

Dory paused and looked around at the many apartments. "Okay, from this point on, we don't go near anymore doors," she announced. "Straight on to the next staircase. No stopping!"

"My shoelace is untied," Winston muttered. His lower lip jutted out and his eyebrows jumped up his forehead in panic.

"Okay, we can pause for that," Dory corrected with a roll of her eyes.

The werewolf bent over to fix the loose lacing on his white tennis shoe. He stretched out the two ends of the laces first, making sure they were even in length. He then wrapped one end around the other, twisting it carefully so that each part of the lacing would be symmetrical. When it was not perfect, Winston took out the knot and started over again. The other three stood around him watching as if the construction of a bow was the most fascinating event in human history. Dory wanted to be annoyed and insist they move on, yet her eyes could not be moved from Winston's precise actions.

Frank hopped out of Dory's arms and padded over to

Winston's face which was hovering over the shoe as he stooped. Thrilled at someone being so close to his level, Frank attempted to lick the man's face. Instantly, Winston ran into a corner of the hallway next to the stairwell. He kept his face to the wall and breathed heavily as if trying to overcome an asthma attack.

"Sorry," Dory said before scolding Frank. The little dog looked back at Winston longing to make the man his new friend. Still, he stayed sitting where he was told and waited patiently for the next command from his mistress.

"You need to relax," Raleigh berated Winston as he settled himself on the floor. Ghost also sat. He mimicked Raleigh's posture, his shoulders slouching and his knees bent upward.

"Guys, get up," Dory groaned. "We need to get going."

"Hey, talk to Fuzzy Wuzzy over there," Raleigh answered, setting his cooler behind him to support his back.

The werewolf released a shuttering sigh and pivoted himself so he was no longer facing the filthy corner. Turning to look at them, Winston sat with his arms crossed over his chest. "What kind of dog is that?" he asked nervously. He was attempting to prove something although he was unsure of what. He stole a determined look at Raleigh who had tilted back his head to feign sleep in lazy cowboy fashion.

Frank tilted his head to one side at the word dog. "He's a Goldendoodle," Dory explained as it if was just the most natural thing to be explaining to an obsessive compulsive werewolf.

"A golden what?" Winston chuckled anxiously.

"Half golden retriever, half poodle," Dory clarified, then reached out to pat Frank on the head. "The best of both halves, right my baby."

Raleigh gagged. "That isn't a dog breed. That sounds

more like a sleazy gentleman's club."

Ghost looked over and laughed. "You surprise me. You act all logical and critical, but you talk to that dog like it's your child."

"Of course," Dory answered aghast at their surprise. With complete seriousness, she added, "Have you seen that fuzzy face? A dog is a girl's best friend."

"And I thought my life was lonely," the Ghost commented teasingly.

With a playful glare, Dory crouched near her dog and commanded, "Frank, sic him."

The dog ran at Ghost and passed through his leg nearly running into the wall as if the spirit was not there at all. Frank then rounded back and sat waiting at Ghost's feet, wagging his tail.

Ghost attempted to pat the dog, letting his clear hand settled atop Frank's head so the little dog could feel the cold air. "Way to follow orders, killer."

Raleigh picked up Frank and waved him at Winston. "See, not scary."

"So says you, but any canine reaction can cause me to have . . . an episode," Winston argued, standing up and attempting to back further into the corner. He noticed a pile of dust bunnies and leaped away. He managed to remain at a safe distance from the dog and others. "I should have stayed at home," he told them in the midst of a low whine.

Trying not to seem condescending, Dory told Winston, "Frank thinks he's a person anyway. I don't think you'll get too many canine vibes from him." She held out her hands and Raleigh handed her the dog. "If you want, I can carry him and try harder to keep him away from you every time you think you're going to go wolf."

Winston edged slightly more out of the corner. "Yeah?" he quietly asked.

"Yeah." Dory offered him a friendly smile. "Are there any other precautions we should take to keep you from changing?"

"Well.... Do you have any silver on you?" Winston asked hesitantly.

"Nope," Dory told him, "Afraid not." She leaned back on her heels and the key in her pocket shifted against her side. "Oh, wait. I think this is silver." Shifting Frank against her right hip so she had a free hand, she pulled out the key. The dim bulb of one of the sconces bounced off the smooth surface of the object and gave the key a sparkly sheen.

Winston reached out his hand and thought about touching a single finger to the key. However, he retracted his hand and shook his head. "I'm just going to trust your judgment. If I start to wolf-out, just make sure you touch me with that. The pain should snap me out of the transformation."

"I don't really want to hurt you though," Dory stated hesitantly.

"You already smacked him once," Ghost corrected. "Don't you mean you don't want to hurt him again?"

"I'll hurt him if you can't do it. Better than being eaten," Raleigh responded with a suspicious glare at Winston.

"And what keeps you from taking a bite out of her?" Ghost challenged to the vampire, feeling bad for the shy werewolf.

"Self control," Raleigh proudly told them.

Winston turned towards the corner once more and hung his head like a punished child. Dory jumped over to him, all the while glaring at Raleigh with a look that read "Nice work, idiot".

Handing Frank off to Raleigh, she crouched near Winston, careful not to touch him due to his obvious feeling of distaste towards germs. "You really shouldn't pay any attention to Raleigh. Seriously, I only just met the guy and I've already figured out when to ignore him. He's just full of hot air."

"He's right though. I'm not very good at controlling myself," Winston incoherently told her through heavy breaths. Dory worried about him having a panic attack, however he continued to speak. "But it's so hard having two sides to yourself. I never know which is going to be when and I'm never really sure what I'm going to do as the wolf."

"There must be something you like about when you change." Dory was not sure why she wanted to comfort him. The despair that radiated from the man's body seemed to quell her eagerness to keep moving. "I mean, you're strong and large and you have those nasty looking claws. I bet you can open cans no problem with those. And no one messes with you, which must be good, since you don't really like people." Winston looked unconvinced. Dory went on by asking again, "What's one thing you like about yourself after you change?"

Winston thought long and hard, looking down at his own rough palms and thinking of how they looked covered in hair, ready to tear into anything that moved. "I like my teeth," he at last divulged.

"Your teeth? Odd choice." Dory hoped his explanation would not have to do with how he kept people away from his apartment.

"When I was a kid, I didn't like to eat meat because I didn't like chewing it," Winston explained, "but with my wolf teeth, chewing up meat isn't a problem."

"Well—" Dory tried her best to keep out the mental image of the great beast eating. "There you go. Good teeth. Keep thinking about that. Remember, you turning into a wolf is not entirely a bad thing."

"I guess so," he said thoughtfully.

Standing up, Dory brushed the hallway dust from her clothes and announced, "Enough stalling. We're wasting time and I'd like to be at the Landlord's before I'm an old woman."

The three rose from the floor, Raleigh setting the puppy down. Frank ran after Dory, staying close to her heels as they moved to the end of the hallway. Winston was the first to start up the stairs. Dory pulled Raleigh aside at the bottom step, out of the werewolf's earshot.

"Way to be sensitive, Raleigh," Dory scolded.

"What do you want from me? I'm a vampire," he argued.

"You want to be something more? You want to feel real caring again? Start practicing now," she sternly told him, "or you can stop hanging around with us." She walked away, yet not before knocking her elbow against his to emphasize her threat.

She stepped up alongside Ghost who noted, "You're not afraid of anything, are you."

"What? Oh, I'm afraid of a lot of things. I just don't tolerate bullying." She said this without much thought.

The two started up the staircase after Winston and Ghost observed, "I thought you were more of a pessimist when I first met you."

"That was only an hour or so ago. And I was . . . scratch that, I am having a bad day. Besides, we can't know everything about each other in an hour."

"Feels like longer than that. With all of these little adventures, it feels like we've been walking for days. Then again, the dead don't have a great sense of time."

She noticed his physical appearance was more solid than normal. She couldn't even see the wall behind him. She tried to feel his arm. Her hand moved down and grasped the edge of his fingers. "I can touch you," she stated with shock.

"Yeah. It comes and goes, every now and again I'm able to move things or hold things," he explained. He smiled and wiggled his fingers a little in her grip.

"Can you feel that?" she asked taking a hold of his palm.

They paused on the steps and Ghost focused on their hands. "Yeah, but I'm not sure if it's me actually feeling you or if it's my somehow remembering what it's like to have someone hold my hand."

"You're getting too technical for me," she said with a laugh.

"I'm just a memory. Raleigh knows what I am. He can probably explain it better than me. I'm an echo left behind so everything I do and say isn't really real." He said the words like a scientist, but Dory heard a hint of melancholy in them.

She gave his hand a squeeze. "Well, you feel pretty real to me."

"Thanks." He smiled back at her and tried to return the pressure on her hand, but his form started to fade out again.

Raleigh grunted at the pair of them as he paused a few steps below. Dory averted the vampire's gaze, then skipped up the steps a little faster in order to catch up with Winston.

Raleigh sped up his own pace. He rolled his pupils at the spirit and whispered, "Ghost. Stop making goo-goo eyes at the human girl. It's not going to happen, pal. You're dead."

"I wasn't," Ghost explained, his tone still clinical. "I was just—"

"Yeah. Whatever." Raleigh grumbled, and then muttered under his breath as the two followed behind Dory.

Winston let out a shout. "We need to go another

way!"

Dory ran further ahead to see what was wrong. "Winston?" she called as she caught up to him. Winston pointed his hairy knuckle at a spot above the stairway. A spider had made its web across the top, stretching from one side of the ceiling to another.

Dory didn't mean to be tactless, but the word "Seriously?" escaped her mouth.

Winston's shoulders slumped. Coming up behind them on the stairs, Raleigh muttered under his breath, "Who's insensitive now?"

"Shut up," she snapped, and then turned to Winston. "I'm sorry. I was just surprised. There are lots of people afraid of spiders. But if you just duck and run, I promise you it isn't going to get you."

"There are at least four types of poisonous spiders in this state alone," Winston rationalized.

"Yes, but they're more interested in flies than they are in werewolves," Ghost pointed out. "They can't exactly wrap you up in their web and suck your blood." Dory shot him a wincing look. "I'm not helping, am I?"

Dory shook her head but continued talking to Winston. "As long as we don't bother the web, that spider won't bother us, got it?"

"You didn't see this spider," Winston corrected pointing upward at the ceiling. "It was bigger than normal spiders; much bigger."

"Of course it was," Raleigh patronizingly responded, swinging his cooler so it hit the back of the werewolf's legs.

Ghost suggested, "You can always pull your shirt over your head and run. That's what you're supposed to do with spiders, right."

"Nope. Killer bees," Dory told him, then noticed a strange scurrying sound. It echoed in the stairwell.

All four looked up and Winston proclaimed with a girly

scream, "Its back!"

A spider, as big as a Doberman, descended from the ceiling. It eyed the travelers and rubbed its eight hairy legs in synchronization against its web. Moving further down, it started to retrace over parts at the bottom of the web. Then, it dropped a little farther and started to add to the trap. Within minutes, the sticky white net covered the stairway and blocked their exit.

"We need to find another way," Winston repeated.

"There is no other way," Raleigh answered, starting back down the stairway. He moved more quickly than the cowardly werewolf.

Ghost and Dory followed, Dory carried Frank who had begun to bark wildly at the new threat. "I didn't know they could get that big," Ghost commented with interest.

"Focus," Dory told him, glancing up the dark staircase at the giant arachnid that waited for them. "I'm adding this to our list of complaints about this building."

"We should get some bug spray," Winston meekly suggested.

"We'd need to bug bomb the whole building to kill that thing," Ghost told him. "All in favor of giving up on this quest?"

"No," Dory insisted, "We're over halfway there. We can't give up now." As if protesting her words the spider shook its pincher at them and reached out one leg. The group backed away further and Dory whined, "Okay, this would all be soooo much easier if the Landlord just had a phone."

"Should I roll up a giant newspaper?" Raleigh joked. "I can start pounding on doors and asking around."

"We aren't really going to try to kill it, are we?" Dory asked, hugging Frank closer to her. "It's huge. How do we kill something like that?"

"Do you have a better idea?" Winston wanted to

know. His shoulders shook as if he were freezing to death.

"I might," Ghost put in, his eyes bright with new excitement. "Winston, can you make those claws of yours ever appear at will?"

"What?! No! Why would I want to change at will?" the werewolf protested. "That's a stupid thing to ask!"

"He's not stupid. He only asked about your claws, not your whole person." Dory defended then lightened her tone. "Just hear out the idea, Winston."

Raleigh, as if sensing Ghost's plan, asked Winston, "Do you think you could do it? Do you think you could transform just your hands?"

The idea sent Winston into a panic. He started to rant, "You can't be serious! Even if I could control this curse . . . which I can't, I'm not going anywhere near that spider. Claws or no claws, whatever your plan is, you can leave me out of it."

"Why don't we listen to the plan, then you can protest," Dory told him, trying not to laugh at his behavior. All the while, she kept her eyes firmly following the four eyes of the giant spider. Each time the arachnid twitched a leg, a chill scurried up Dory's spine. She'd never been scared of bugs, but the sight of each black marble focusing upon her turned her knees to pudding.

Ghost explained, "I can distract it, right. I'm sure that thing will be pretty confused by something it can walk right through. While I'm keeping the spider busy, Winston can use his claws to cut down the web. Then Raleigh, you can help pull it down and Dory will run through."

Her wobbly legs were instantly forgotten. "Wait, that's all I do in this brilliant plan? Run?" Dory wrinkled her nose and made a "humph" sound. "I can help you know. This isn't the Middle Ages."

Raleigh shook his head, glancing up the stairway where the spider awaited them. "No. Ghost is right.

Winston and I aren't human. I doubt the spider venom will kill us. But you would probably die instantly. It's safer if you and Frank just run through."

"And act as moral support," Ghost added with a grin.

"Yeah, I guess," Dory grumbled with disappointment. She rested her face in the soft curls of Frank's fur and grumbled in the dog's ear, "Behind every great man is a woman telling him how dumb he is."

Winston jutted out his bottom jaw and talked over his lower teeth, looking a little like a piranha. "Are you guys forgetting something? This plan won't work because I'm not helping you. I can't change my hands into claws at will and I am not going near that spider." The werewolf began to pout as he stared up at the spider. The creature had stopped moving in order to stare back patiently.

Ghost glanced back and forth between the werewolf and the little dog in Dory's arms. With the eager glint still shining in his eyes, the translucent man said, "I bet you anything that I can only make your hands change."

Winston backed up against one of the apartment doors, his face in a perfect twisted grimace. "What? No!"

"Oh, come on," Raleigh coaxed, his own fingers shaking slightly as the spider shifted its weight and the web trembled. "Live a little. Take the bet."

"I'm trying to stay alive here which is why I will not take that bet," Winston insisted, "You will just have to do it without me."

Dory settled on the dusty hallway floor, feeling that this would take a while, with Frank on her lap. She watched the nervous Winston start to sway back and forth. For a moment, she thought that he would dash down the hallway and back to his apartment, never to emerge again. When he at last froze, she took the opportunity to say, "Aren't you at least curious to see if it works? Think about it. If Ghost can get only one part of you to turn into a wolf then that means you're one step closer to having some control over your powers."

Edging a little further back towards the group, Winston asked, "Do you really think so?"

"Can't hurt to try," she told him flippantly.

"What if I go completely wolf?" he questioned, rubbing the back of his neck.

Raleigh swiftly responded, speaking with the pomp of a soldier from an old melodrama, "I won't let you hurt anyone. I'll restrain you against a wall somehow if I have to or lock you in the bathroom of one of these apartments."

The vow won Winston over. His own fear of Raleigh's powers left him confident that the vampire would be able to stop him from any regrettable acts. He stepped back over to the group. "Okay. Ghost, how are we going to do this?"

Ghost clapped his hands together. However, the sound was faint as if someone had clapped from another room. "Great! All right, Winston. Shut your eyes."

"What? Why?" Winston instantly demanded to know, his shoulders tensing.

"Never question a scientist in the middle of an experiment," Ghost told him. "Now, trust me and shut your eyes."

First, Winston glanced at Dory who offered an encouraging smile. He closed his eyes, waiting for further instructions.

Ghost waved his hands in front of Winston's face to check his vision. "Good. Now what do you think about to try and stay human?"

"Pudding," Winston answered simply.

Raleigh laughed, "Why pudding?"

With his eyes still shut tight, Winston explained, "When I change, I don't usually want pudding, just meat, but whenever I change back, I crave it."

"Oh," Raleigh replied. The noncommittal noise had the undertone of criticism until Ghost made a rolling motion with this left hand. Raleigh understood and went on with a much more interested, "Oh? Really? That's cool. So, uh, what kind of pudding do you usually want?"

As Winston began to list flavors, Ghost took the opportunity to whisper in Dory's ear. She stood up to listen carefully to his suggestion, and then followed it exactly. On tiptoe, she walked over to Winston with Frank still in her arms. The little dog wagged his tail and wriggled as the approached the man that smelled like a canine. She held out Frank, hovering him in front of Winston's right hand which hung limply at his side as he began to give a detailed description of the consistency of a perfect pudding. Frank was thrilled to be so close to Winston. He licked the back of the young man's hand and pushed his nose against his index finger.

Winston instantly flinched and opened his eyes. Dory moved away with Frank, whose tail had stopped waving, realizing that he was not getting the chance to actually play with the giant man-dog. Winston's right hand transformed. The fingers stretched and fur sprouted from his skin. What had been fingernails expanded into tiny bone daggers at the ends of his digits. The rest of Winston remained the same. He pointed one of the long claws at Ghost with amazement. "How did you know it would work?"

"I didn't," Ghost said truthfully. "It was just a theory. I was thinking of your transformation as more of an allergy. People have been known to ignore their allergies and not even realize they are having a reaction. I thought if Frank touched your hand when you weren't paying attention, then maybe only your hand would change, like someone who rubs their eyes after playing with a cat or gets a rash from touching a mold they aren't supposed to."

"That's really neat," Raleigh awed as he held up

Winston's furry hand for inspection. "Do think that would work for sunlight too?"

Ghost frowned then faded in and out. "I doubt it and I wouldn't try it."

Dory stole a peek up the staircase. The giant arachnid had built its web down to the floor and was sitting on the steps waiting for them. She had to admit, the web was beautiful, a giant symmetrical pattern which caught the tint from the hallway's florescent lighting and seemed to shine with glitter. "I know this is a big moment for you, Winston, but that spider is spreading his web even further. Are we ready to face it?" Dory asked impatiently.

Raleigh and Ghost both answered, "Yes" at the same time that Winston answered, "No."

Ghost started up the stairs. "Too late now, Winston," he called over his shoulder. "Get ready to take down that web."

The spider had climbed back into its trap, hiding amongst the shadows on the ceiling. Ghost strolled up to the wispy net and pretended to be stuck. He stood perfectly still against the edge of the web, feeling the delicate, gummy strands moving through his body. "Oh no," he pretended to be frightened. Ghost was not a very good actor. Each word came out like a separate sentence and his voice held no inflection. "I have been caught in a spider web. What am I going to do?"

His horrible performance fooled the spider who began to descend, fangs clicking and legs twitching. Winston and Raleigh stood on either side of the staircase, ready to run up at the right moment.

"I don't like this," Winston whimpered.

"Oh come on," Raleigh said with a smile, swinging the cooler in his hands back and forth anxiously. "You're here. Might as well enjoy it."

As the spider fell upon Ghost, it slackened the line of

web coming from its back end. It moved directly through the young man, landing in an awkward position and breaking one of its eight limbs with a pop. Furious, but not understanding what was happening, the spider reached out a front leg which swept through Ghost's chest. He ran to one side of the staircase and waited for the spider to attempt to corner him. As Ghost distracted the spider against one wall, Raleigh and Winston sprinted along the other side of the staircase, directly behind the spider's bulbous body.

Winston reached up his clawed hand and began to slice at the webbing where it stuck to the walls. The white filaments gathered on the ends of his fingers, but cut easily like scissors through hair. Every few slashes of his claw caused Winston to cringe in disgust and try to shake the bits of web off the ends of his fingers. "This isn't sanitary," he hissed at Raleigh who was busy trying not to get caught in the strong center of the web.

With a roll of his eyes, Raleigh used the edge of his shirt to wipe off Winston's claws. "Stop whining. Would you rather be spider chow?" He tossed his cooler up the stairs through the small hole they had started to cut in the web. It landed on its side with a dull thud.

As Winston and Raleigh cut enough of the webbing away from one wall for a person to slip through, Dory crept up behind them with Frank in her arms. The spider was still contending with Ghost, who was smugly darting up and down the stairs, allowing the spider's legs to move through his body. He chuckled slowly. "That's right, you big eight legged idiot, you just keep trying to catch me." He glanced over at Dory from over the top of the spider's body. He winked at her and she smiled back. As Frank wagged his tail at Ghost, the young man didn't realize that he had become solid. The spider once again slapped one leg at its prey, sweeping Ghost's legs out from under him. Ghost fell over himself and rolled down the stairs.

The spider turned to watch him hit the bottom step and noticed the young woman pinned between itself and the wall. Dory froze and attempted to hold Frank against her side, hiding the small animal from the giant bug.

"Run!" Winston yelled back at her as a large chunk of web fell down on his head. "Ahh! Sticky!" he cried out.

Ghost struggled to stand up while Raleigh took the opportunity to jump down onto the spider's back. He punched at one of the eyes causing the eye to burst like a water balloon. Winston watched, looking ready to vomit until someone shouted at him to finish cutting a hole in the web. Ghost ran at the spider's back legs, pulling on one of them with as much force as he could manage. Still, despite injuries and annoyances, the spider persisted towards its new prey, trapping Dory between two legs and the wall.

She thought about trying to hit the spider, but the pincers moving back and for within its mouth kept her still, tossing Frank onto the step. The little dog hesitated to leave her. Then, with a whistle from Winston, ran up the stairs and through the hole in the web. Dory sighed with relief as Frank vanished up to the next floor. Turning back to the spider, she shut her eyes tightly and waited for it to sink its fangs into her skin.

The spider suddenly bucked backwards and waved its arms around frantically. Dory, Ghost, and Winston all looked in time to see Raleigh remove his own teeth from the spider's back, then wipe his mouth on the back of his hand.

"Blech!" he yelled, then felt a confidant surge as the spider scurried up the wall to hide in the shadows of the ceiling. "Yeah! See how you like it, you overgrown—" He paused and took a deep breath, "Okay. I can't think of a good insult. Let's just go!"

They ran through the hole in the web in single file, and

then paused at the top of the stairs to make certain the monster would not follow.

Staring down into the dark steps, the vampire shuddered. "That is possibly the most disgusting thing I've ever done in my undead life," Raleigh stated as he spit down the stairs. He twisted up his face in further revolt. "Oh, nasty! I hope this flavor isn't permanent." He pointed a finger at Dory. "You owe me, big time!" He then reached into his cooler. He pulled a plastic plasma bag hurriedly to his lips and began to slurp.

Ghost smiled at the vampire jokingly. "Oh, come on, Raleigh. I hear bugs are full of protein."

"Thanks, guys." Dory simply hugged each of them with a feeling of sheer joy. As she pulled away from Raleigh, who was the last in her line of hugs, she said, "Okay, that was the only mush we're going to have for today. Let's get moving."

Winston's claws retracted and the fur receded back into his skin. The moment his hands were human again, he jumped ahead of the others and lead the way to the seventh floor hallway.

Chapter Eight:
    The Seventh Floor; The Journey is Stopped

Winston rounded a corner at the top of the stairs and entered the hallway first, hopping up and down. "I have to go," he told the others with a whimper.

"If you want to go home, I understand," Dory told him as met him on the seventh floor.

"No," he said with a small amount of embarrassment. "I have to go. I need to pee."

"You mean that spider actually scared the crap out of you," Raleigh joked as he and Ghost were the last to follow.

"Not funny," Winston whined dancing a little more urgently.

"Well, it's not like there's a public restroom in an apartment building," Dory said. "Why don't you run back down to your place, go, and then meet us back here."

"Go back down? By myself? I don't want to find out what else is on that last floor, especially by myself." Winston crossed one leg over the other and continued to hop.

"Just don't think about it," Ghost told him. "And don't think about water in any form."

"Why did you say that? Now I'm thinking about water, all forms of water. I can't hold it."

"You're a wolf. Go in the corner," Raleigh said in as close to a helpful tone as he could manage.

"That's disgusting!" Winston bellowed. "Even when I'm having an episode, I never go on the floor. I'm the werewolf equivalent of paper trained."

"I don't really want to think about that," Raleigh muttered as he tossed his cooler around like a basketball.

Dory pointed down the hallway to an ajar entrance. "There's an open apartment door. We can ask whoever owns it if you can use their bathroom."

"I thought we weren't going into any more apartments," Ghost said with caution.

"Do you want him to go on the floor?" Dory asked, "Or go all the way back down to his home? Winston's right about one thing. We need to keep moving forward. If not we might never get anywhere. Besides, we'll be quick. How long could it take for him to pee?"

The four people and the puppy were careful in how they approached the partially open door. Raleigh pushed it open with his foot and the group was met with an empty room. A window provided light, which Raleigh hid from. No furniture. No decorations. The walls were white, waiting to be painted over by a new owner. Even the kitchen was missing the basic appliances of a refrigerator or an oven.

Winston burst in and headed back to the open bedroom. He slammed the bathroom door and they heard him release a relieved sigh. Dory stepped into the family room, Frank was close behind her. "This is nicer than our place," she commented. "She bounced a little on her heels, letting her feet repeatedly sink into the floor." Even the carpet is softer."

Ghost followed her in and surveyed the area. "Looks like everything was just re-done. New counters in the kitchen and a new lock on the window."

"The window locks! The window in my apartment doesn't lock!" Dory said with indignation.

Winston came out from the bathroom, water dripping from his fingers. "There's no soap," he told them with despair.

Frank, circled a spot four times, settled down on the floor, and fell asleep. Dory watched him with a shake of her head. "I'll have to carry him," she said.

Winston shrugged. "I could use a quick sit down. My legs are still shaking from the spider attack." He glanced out into the hallway where the vampire was pacing. "What's Raleigh doing?"

"Sunlight can kill him," Dory explained.

"Oh." Winston squirmed around the room a little, then decidedly pulled his shirt over his head. He hung the shirt from the window frame, blocking the direct sun rays but still allowing light in the room. "You can come in now," he called to Raleigh with his arms self-consciously crossed over his chest.

The vampire inched into the room carefully. He waited until he was entirely inside, patting at his arms and squinting his eyes as if waiting for his skin to break out in bursts of flames. Finally, he relaxed. "Okay, cool."

The door suddenly slammed. The sound of wood hitting wood caught their attention. They turned to see the entrance vanish into the wall; gone completely as if a door had never been there. Each of them ran at it, like their panic could somehow make the exit reappear.

"Not cool," Winston corrected, his hands turning to claws and ripping at the door. Each mark he made instantly vanished. "Can't breathe! Walls closing in!" The werewolf began to mutter, backing towards a corner.

Raleigh asked with confusion, "You're claustrophobic? You didn't leave your apartment for years!"

"That was different," Winston argued, panting heavily. "I could leave whenever I wanted."

"But you didn't," Ghost commented. He inspected the place where the door had been and waved a distracted hand back at Winston. "Just pretend this is just like that."

"How?" Winston whined.

Ghost thought long and hard, and then simply answered, "Try."

Dory went to the window. "Raleigh, hide in the bathroom." He followed her instruction as she pulled down Winston's yellow shirt and tossed it back at the flustered werewolf. After turning the lock latch, she tugged and pushed upward at the frame. Her fingers strained against the wood, her nails aching as they pressed against the window. "It's stuck!"

Ghost tried to stick his head through the wall where the door was and hit his forehead. Following the thud, he gasped. "Am I solid right now?"

Dory moved over to him, her hand outstretched. Her fingers went directly through his upper arm. She looked up at his faint face at the wall behind him. "No. I can barely see you."

"This place appears to be ghost proof," Raleigh called from the bathroom.

"And the window won't open," Dory restated.

Ghost peered out at the skinny ledge by pressing his head against the glass. "Even if you could get out the window, there's no place to go except a seven story drop."

"Is there any way out through the bedroom?" Dory wondered aloud.

"Not unless you can fit through a six inch vent," Winston murmured, settling himself against a wall. Each of them sat, sighing heavily. Frank tried to crawl into Ghost's lap, but fell directly through the man. Upset by this, the little dog ran to Dory, curled up against her leg, and fell back asleep.

"Now what do we do?" Dory grumbled.

"Wait till the sun goes down," Raleigh called from the bathroom. He was sitting in the tub as if it were a sofa, leaning his head back against the faucet. In order to occupy himself, the vampire started to drum at the porcelain with his fingertips and the edge of his ruby ring, keeping the beat as he hummed death themed rock songs.

So they waited. Every now and again a conversation would start, usually based around some new phobia of Winston's, who had put his shirt back on while keeping the collar close to his chin. As the room grew darker and the sun vanished, Raleigh came out to sit with them.

Dory glanced up at the moon beginning to appear in the sky. Her voice was a swirl of tact and trepidation as she asked, "Winston, is there a full moon tonight? Or is whole thing just a myth?"

"Sort of." He continued to wrap his neck up in the collar of his polo shirt. "It'll be full tomorrow night. That just means I have even less control over my transformation and even less memory of what I do after I transform." His own stomach growled. "What about you, Raleigh?" He looked over at the vampire while scooting away. "Do you feel any urge to . . . eat?"

Realizing he had left his cooler in the hallway, Raleigh decided he didn't want to worry anyone. "I ate before we left and after the spider. I should be fine till morning," Raleigh told them, his voice full of truth despite his own doubts.

"What happens in the morning?" Winston anxiously wished he hadn't asked.

"I'll feed again and then I'll be fine." Raleigh made it sound so simple.

Winston swallowed hard. "Feed on what?"

"I'll worry about that tomorrow," the vampire nonchalantly replied.

Dory watched them both, trying to feel the danger she was in, yet unable to comprehend it. It seemed difficult to imagine the vicious creatures they could become when looking at them in their worn out, relaxed state.

"Winston, what worries you the most about being a

werewolf?" she asked, leaning forward a bit with interest. Her movement disturbed Frank who demanded to be pet after having been woken. He knocked his head against her hand until she stroked his fur.

"Oh, bring on the can of worms," Raleigh grumbled, lying out on his side with his head propped up on his hand.

Ghost looked encouragingly at Winston. "Actually, I'm curious about that as well."

The man at last released the collar of his shirt in order to think. He rubbed at his stubbled jaw and scratched at his thick head of hair. At last, Winston muttered, "I worry about that theory that a werewolf instinctively kills the thing it loves most."

"I'm fairly positive Hollywood made that one up," Dory told him with understanding. "I think you'll be fine."

"I think it's safer just to stay away from people altogether," Winston went on. "Besides, relationships are terrifying."

"That's not a werewolf thing, that's just a guy thing," Dory teased. "Men and women have very different definitions of love." She thought back on her many boyfriends over the years that she had pushed away and the friends she had barely any contact with any longer, wondering if she should really be giving relationship advice.

"Wait, I'm confused," Ghost put in. "Are werewolves supposed to kill what they love the most in a romantic capacity or just something they love the most like a friend or a pet?"

Winston sat up a little straighter at that question. "Um . . . I'm not sure." He scratched his chin again and grumbled, "That's complicated."

"Love usually is, so I hear," Ghost responded knowingly.

"I was in love once," Raleigh confessed out of the blue. "Right before I was . . . before I became what I am now."

"Really?" Dory stared intently at the lounging vampire. "And she couldn't love a vampire?"

"No. She still loved me, she said." Raleigh hung his head, scratching at his nose and tapping a finger against his chest where his heart used to beat. "She said I just didn't love her the same way anymore."

"Didn't you?"

"I don't know. After I changed I had trouble telling the difference," he replied woefully.

Dory was careful about how she worded her next question. "Is that why you want to have human emotions again? So you can love her?"

He shook his head and dropped his hands into his lap. "No. Oh no. Well, as long as we're having share time, I'll tell the whole story. She's long since gone. I was there when she passed away; a woman of sixty who drifted off in her sleep leaving behind a loving husband, two children, and a brand new grandchild." He began to twist and twine his fingers together as he analyzed himself. "I think . . . I think I want to be able to feel again in memory of her. Before she died, she said she could almost see it in me, the man that I used to be with all the human caring and sadness. She said she wished I could be happy and that somehow I could be that man again." He disentangled his fingers, sat up, and slapped his hands onto his knees. "So I try for her. And for myself. But it's not easy."

Dory nodded, thinking on how sour she had become towards her friends like Maud that had no time for her, yet she still yearned to hear from. "Emotions never are. Can I ask you what her name was?"

Raleigh got up and sat down next to Dory. He pulled out an old fob watch, from his pocket. Opening it, he showed off the sepia toned photo of a pretty, bright haired woman in a light colored dress. Her eyes shone at the camera, full of caring. "Georgiana," he told her with a smile on his lips. "Sweetest woman to ever walk the face of the earth."

Ghost asked, "Do you regret becoming a vampire and not sharing your life with her?"

"Hmm..." Raleigh squinted an eye as he thought. "I'm immortal. We don't really harbor the regret the same way mortals do. It's more like a heart murmur. You know it's there and that someday it's going to hurt you, but for the time being you live with it like it's nothing." He nudged Dory with his shoulder. "What about you? Any big heartbreaks?" He whispered this, as if to have a private conversation with the young woman.

Ghost peered over at them while he listened. Winston also listened, but kept his head down discreetly.

"Everyone has one big heartbreak," Dory answered with a no nonsense shrug.

"Well, I shared mine. Let's hear it," Raleigh requested.

Dory started off in a serious tone. "Well, his name was Nico. He was very cute, very nice, and he acted like he adored me. We did everything together. It was one of those summer romances. You know, the kind where you're afraid that if you aren't constantly together you'll somehow stop feeling the way you do."

"Uh huh," Raleigh said with interest. "Was it one of those hot and heavy love affairs?"

With a secretive tone, Dory answered, "In a way . . . But then, he completely broke my heart."

"What happened?" Raleigh sat up straighter, earnestly listening.

"He pushed me in the mud and called me a stupid head so his friends would stop teasing him." All three of the men's' faces turned to confusion. At last, Dory's face broke into a smile. "We were ten and it was at summer camp."

Ghost laughed and Winston took a turn at rolling his eyes.

"You said it was hot and heavy," Raleigh complained with obvious disappointment.

"Well yeah! It was a hot day and I was wearing a heavy knapsack when he pushed me over," Dory told them all with a giggle, tickled by their expressions. "Really, he was technically my first boyfriend and my first kiss. And the experience left me bitter at summer camps for years after."

"Kissing followed by bitterness," Winston remarked sourly. "Yep, sounds like a first love."

Ghost knitted his brow. "Is it always like that?"

"Not always," Raleigh explained. "For example, your first love must have been okay if this conversation didn't trigger some bitterness in you."

"I have no memories of my life," Ghost reminded. "I don't even know who my first love was so how I can I know if I was bitter or not?"

Raleigh shook his head knowingly. "Trust me. Bitterness survives amnesia. Even if you don't know what you're bitter about, it's there."

"That's an awful theory," Dory commented.

"It's not a theory," he went on, "I've met plenty of my kind who have given themselves amnesia. They've purposely blocked out their own lives but certain things still trigger bitterness or happiness in them, they just don't know the reason."

"Ha!" Dory pointed out triumphantly. "You said happiness too. So happiness is just as strong as bitterness."

"Yeah, but that feeling doesn't last nearly as long," Raleigh told her truthfully. Dory found she couldn't argue with him there.

Winston uncomfortably wiggled where he sat. "I can't really talk. I haven't had a girlfriend in years. I did try dating another werewolf through an online service . . . but she wanted to meet. I had to end it there."

Raleigh got back up and sat down next to Winston.

"Okay, pal. Repeat after me, girls are not scary. Girls are good, especially girls of your own kind."

"But she wanted me to go outside," Winston pointed out.

"Was her profile photo hot?" Raleigh wanted to know.

"Yes," Winston admitted with a faint smile.

Raleigh threw his arms in the air. "Then you go outside! For the love of God, man, you go outside!"

Dory thought about commenting that often people didn't put their real photos for online dating sites, but decided against it. Anything to get Winston to be less afraid of people. She rose and moved over to the window. The world outside of the apartment building was quiet. People were disappearing into their homes. She yawned, wishing she could be in her old place with the spacious living room and cozy bedroom, tucked into her bed with Frank at her feet.

Dory's eyelids drooped then shot back up. In an attempt to stay awake, she pinched her arm and shook her head. "We should each take watch in case this is trap for some beast to come out and eat us. I can do it first if you want."

Ghost turned to her with amusement, then shot Raleigh a knowing look as the vampire let out a laugh. "You forget that we aren't human, don't you?"

She wrinkled her nose thoughtfully, trying to imagine herself back at Kansas Heights in the evening, when the sun streamed through her clean windows and the sounds of happy children left the park across the street. One of her neighbors would be baking and the smell of chocolate chip cookies could lull her into a relaxed state. Dory could almost feel the warmth from her fireplace.

Somewhere in the midst of Dory's daydreaming about her old apartment, Winston had curled up on the floor. He was snoring loudly, his leg kicking like a little puppy dreaming of chasing rabbits.

Raleigh called out over Dory's musings, "Did you hear what I said? We're not human. You sleep. I need to just rest a little and Ghost doesn't need sleep."

"What? You never sleep? Ever" Dory asked Ghost with concern.

"I'm dead. If I slept I couldn't be called a restless spirit," he explained.

"And vampires?" she asked Raleigh incredulously. "That coffin in your apartment is for sleeping in, isn't it?"

"Course it is," Raleigh told her. "And when I'm injured I need rest more than a regular day, but I really don't have to sleep. Although, I probably should tonight. It'll keep me from having to feed as soon."

"You never really answered Winston's question about what you're going to feed on." Ghost eyed him with distrust. He moved closer to Dory as if his non-corporal from could somehow protect the young woman from vampire fangs.

Raleigh made an annoyed face. "I told you before. I've all but kicked the habit of human blood. Yesterday was a minor setback due to the sun burn, but really, Dory and Winston have nothing to worry about from me. I really do prefer animal blood. Especially wild animals, less toxins. When I was going through my human blood rehabilitation, I traveled the world tasting species from all over. Nears in Canada. Lions in Africa. Tigers in India. Goats in the Alps..." As he named off his favorite foods, the vampire started to drift off.

Ghost quickly promised Raleigh, "I'll wake you up before the sun rises."

"Thanks, pal," Raleigh muttered sleepily as he rolled onto his back. He set his hands across his chest and closed his eyes.

Ghost watched Dory look out the window at the

moonlight. She was still thinking of her old apartment, remembering quiet neighbors and her wide kitchen. Only the uneasy sense of being watched kept her in reality.

When Ghost leaned in, cold air clung to her and she rubbed her arms instinctively. "Why is changing the lease so important? Why don't you want to live here for more than three months?"

She turned her eyes away from the unbreakable glass. "I'd think after all that's happened that would be obvious," Dory stated. "I mean, look at where we are. My old apartment never had vampires, werewolves, or ghosts."

"Sounds boring," Ghost commented. "And how do you know none of your neighbors were any of those things? Did you know all your neighbors?"

"No, but I at least saw them all in the daytime and during full moons. And I couldn't see through any of them."

"Okay, okay, you made your point," Ghost answered, yet seemed unconvinced. "But you wanted the lease changed before you knew all of us existed. What's the real reason?"

Dory told him without shame. "I'm just here temporarily until my old apartment gets renovated."

"And this old apartment was a good place?" he asked. "Better than here?"

"It was the best! It was pretty and roomy and close to my parents' house, but not that far from my work—" Dory realized she was babbling and slowed down her speech pattern. "Look, I'm very picky. I lived in seven different dorm rooms during four years of college because none of them ever felt right. My old apartment was the first place that really felt like home since I moved out of my childhood house."

"This place feels like home to me," Ghost said, "and I can't remember my childhood house. I can't even remember my childhood."

"Yeah, but you're a ghost and this place is freaky. You should feel at home. If you didn't live here, you'd have to be set up on some castle parapet sneaking into the background of tourist's photos."

"Is that scary?" Ghost wanted to know.

"No. It just causes lots of people to argue over photography fraud," she clarified, then added with a little blush. "You were kind of scary in the way you were staring at me a minute ago."

He laughed. "Okay. From now I'm just going to stare at every person we meet until they get so nervous they go nuts."

"You're trying to drive them nuts now? I thought you just wanted to scare people?" Dory set a hand on her hip and shook her head at Ghost.

"If it's that easy to frighten people where all I have to do is stare at them I might as well up the stakes," Ghost decided, "What do you think?"

"I think you should go back to practicing your boo," she replied. "And no more staring at me."

"I think you should get some sleep," Ghost told her. He set one hand on her shoulder. The weight was not there, but Dory could feel the chill, like when her dad used press ice cold soda cans directly against her arm. She shivered and he removed his hand. "Sorry."

Behind a little smile, Dory told him, "It's okay." She could see regret in Ghost's eyes, a certain lost expression. She wondered if that came from not knowing how to be dead. She nestled down against the wall, crossing her arms over her chest and closing her eyes. "Good night, Ghost."

"You sure you can sleep in a room with a werewolf, vampire, and an extra spooky spirit?" he asked, referring to himself in a dramatic tone.

Dory opened one eye and smirked, "The werewolf is terrified of being a werewolf, the vampire is well fed, and you're . . . you. I think I'm safe." She motioned for Frank who curled up in her lap before she shut her eyes again. "So, I repeat, goodnight Ghost."

"Good night, Dory," he replied.

Ghost watched over the other three and the little dog until the sun rose again. When he was solid, he took the opportunity to find a sheet of cardboard in the bedroom closet. He set it over the window so the light wouldn't hurt Raleigh. It was still early in the morning when the werewolf, vampire, and girl slowly woke up.

At first, the morning was awkward, each of them ignoring their hunger and taking another attempt at searching for a way out. After an hour or so they gave up. The group of them stood around the room, boredom setting in. Dory paced while the three guys made unhelpful comments.

"You could leave this building if you wanted, but you don't," Ghost restated, looking at Winston skeptically, "I don't even remember what's out there but I'd leave in a heartbeat if I could . . . and if I still had a heartbeat. Isn't there anything in the rest of the world you miss?"

Winston shrugged. "Not really. It was all crowded and noisy and dirty. People always pushing and shoving. There were so many of them too. Sometimes I'd be standing on the street and I'd catch the scent of just the right one. Certain smells trigger it and I'd go wolf. I don't miss that temptation."

"Come on, man," Raleigh put in, "There are days I even miss sunlight and I hated the heat!"

Thinking over the subject, Winston slapped his knee decidedly. "I miss seeing movies on the big screen," he announced. "There's always something different about seeing it in theaters instead of on TV. I mean sure there aren't any commercials, but just the feel of a movie is different that way, you know what I mean?"

Ghost shook his head. "I can remember what movie theaters are and I can get little snippets in my head of stuff I probably saw when I was alive, but the details are sketchy."

"I remember going to the movies when Technicolor was a big deal," Raleigh explained. "I had a thing for Vivian Leigh . . . and the Blue Fairy in Pinocchio, but that doesn't leave this room."

"She was indeed a hot transparent chick," Winston gruffly replied.

"We need to find someone like that for Ghost," Raleigh suggested. "You remember that film, buddy?"

Ghost scratched his head. "The cartoon?"

"That's the one."

"You want to set me up with a cartoon?" Edging away from Raleigh, he gruffly added, "And still the best offer I can ever remember getting." He seemed more solid as he tried to hide his own embarrassment.

Winston and Raleigh began to heckle him. "Sometimes TV women are the best kind," Winston joked. Dory wrinkled her nose disgustedly at the comment. Frank followed her restless pace.

Raleigh added, "I guess in life you didn't meet any women worth remembering."

"Ugh!" Dory exclaimed, "Enough! Leave him alone, you two. You're just jealous because you wish you could forget all the girls who ever rejected you."

Leaning in towards Dory, his fangs flashing and his eyes catching her gaze, Raleigh smoothly replied, "No girl ever rejected me."

She stared him down, her lips forming a stern line. "Without your vampire powers?"

"Oh, I always had the power of charm," he answered, then motioned to Winston and Ghost in search of the usual expression guys gave one another to back each other up.

Giving Winston a sharp glance, then turning back to Raleigh she turned her voice harsh yet quiet. "Let me try a different approach. You are the oldest one here. How about, instead of acting like a pig, you be a good role model for those of us who are scared, confused, and just want to go home. If you really want to earn back some human caring, start with this group right here." Both her arms flailed about her, slicing angrily at the air. The change in her tone caused Frank to wander away; worried that he was somehow in trouble.

Her words and expression withered Raleigh. He noticed Ghost's vision avoiding his own and Winston's discomfort with Dory's annoyance. The vampire closed his mouth to cover his fangs and muttered, "Sorry. You have to remember, it's been a while since I've been around people in a social capacity."

"Me too," Winston piped up.

"Me three," Ghost answered.

"I'm not mad at you, Ghost," Dory told him.

"Oh, good," Ghost replied, "I was trying to figure out what I'd done."

Raleigh waved Winston over to his side of the room. "Come on. Let's see if we can find another way out of here."

Ghost approached Dory and asked in a whisper, "Were you just standing up for me?"

Dory ducked her head and mumbled, "No." She then looked up at him and shrugged, "Okay, yes. Well, more for women everywhere. I need to stand up for my gender amongst all this testosterone and teeth and fur and see-throughedness."

Ghost watched her carefully and wondered out loud, "Do your other friends make you this aggravated?"

The question instantly struck a nerve. Dory crossed her arms over her chest and growled, "Boy, I'm starting to get sick of being the only human in this group."

Ignoring her sniping, Ghost gave a hearty laugh and attempted to place a hand on her shoulder as he'd done the night before, only to have it slip through and down the inside of her arm. Quickly retracting his hand he told her, "You still have Frank, who thinks he's human, right."

"Good point," Dory responded then glanced around the room, "Wait a second." Her voice turned to a panic and her heart raced, "Where is Frank?" Not a single curly hair of the little dog could be seen.

Ghost ran over to Winston and Raleigh. "Guys, the dog is gone."

"How? There's no way out of here," Winston pointed out.

"Well, obviously, Frank found a way. Help us look for him," Ghost explained with frustration, then began to call to the little dog.

The other two joined in while Dory began to circle the room. "Where could he be?"

"Don't worry, we'll find him," Raleigh gently told her. Then, he whispered to Winston and Ghost while moving them as far from Dory as possible, "Do you realize how depressed she'll be if we don't find him?"

"It's not like he could go far," Winston put in. "Unless something came in here and took him. You don't think—"

"We would've seen something or at least heard him. I think this is the quietest Frank's been since I met those two," Ghost put in. "I'm going to try poking my head into some of the walls. Maybe he found a hole in the boards or a vent to hide in or something."

"You've already tried that," Raleigh said. "You can't go through these walls, remember."

Ghost waved his finger at the family room and kitchen walls. "Not these walls," he said.

A loud thud from within cupboards in the kitchen

caught everyone off guard. Dory rushed in. "You dumb-dumb, did you get yourself locked in a cupboard?" she cooed. Her hands reached out for the cheap wooden door of a lower cabinet when the entire room trembled violently.

The cupboard doors rattled. Soon, the entire wall cracked across the middle and opened wide. A set of sharp teeth were revealed as the facade of the cabinets folded along the floor and ceiling. They clapped once at Dory who let out a shriek. Raleigh hissed at the wall and pulled Dory out of the way. Winston ran to the wall where the door had been. His hands cracked and reformed into claws which scratched futilely until blood trickled from his fur.

The teeth scraped against one another and a fowl breath permeated the apartment. "I think we woke it up," Ghost murmured.

Winston's sickly voice could barely be heard above the growling of the walls. "Woke what up?"

"The apartment. I think no monsters live in here because this is the monster." Sensing Ghost's words, the floor beneath them started to shift and shake, attempting to edge them towards the kitchen. As the giant teeth making up the whole of the wall gnashed and slobbered, he added, "And it is hungry."

Dory's hands flew to her mouth in horror. "Oh no! Frank!"

"No, Dory, I don't think it got him. We would have heard it—"

The kitchen started to snap its jaws more violently. Winston fell over. He scrambled back to the rest of the group, clawing at the carpet to keep himself moving.

"How are we supposed to get out of here?" Dory gasped out each word with her arms stretched out on either side of her. She danced around to keep her balance on the rumbling floor.

"I'll try putting my head through another wall," Ghost explained as he edged away from the kitchen.

Raleigh, his eyes ablaze with fear, shouted back, "Like I said, you already tried that!"

"But I never tried in there!" Ghost ran into the bedroom and the others trailed close behind him. Winston stayed so close at his heels, his own feet went straight through Ghost's.

Going to the wall which separated the room from the hallway, Ghost stuck out his hands in front of him. Everyone held their breath as Ghost approached the wall. His hand slipped though the plaster as if there was nothing there.

His head poked through next. Sitting patiently in the hallway on the other side of the wall sat Frank, wagging his tail excitedly. "Dory, I found your dog!"

"Really!" Without a thought, Dory followed Ghost and practically fell through the wall. Winston and Raleigh ran after her.

"Was this a wall? I mean, was this wall solid before?" asked Raleigh as he passed his hand back through the wall. It tingled a little like he was holding his hand in a freezer.

"I can't remember if we checked it," Winston admitted afraid to go close to the wall as if it would grab him and pull him back into the room.

Scrambling to her feet and collecting Frank into her arms, Dory stated "What does it matter? We're out now."

Raleigh seemed a little stunned. He combed the hall, but his cooler of blood had vanished. Giving up the search with his mouth agape, Raleigh moved closer to Dory, his eyes glazed over. "Yes. Out now." The repeated words sounded dazed and far away. He moved a hand out to touch Dory where her shoulder met her slender neck.

She bat his hand away fearlessly and said, "Let's get upstairs before our hunger gets the better of us." She glanced at Raleigh whose empty stomach caused him to snarl at the girl.

Instinctively, Winston and Ghost stood between the vampire and Dory. Raleigh continued to growl as they tried to create a barrier. The vampire's shoulders tensed and he puffed out his chest like a rooster. "I'm not going to hurt her," he tried to convince them.

"All the same, I think you better walk behind us for a bit," Ghost stated. "Dory, you go in front."

Calming down, Raleigh said, "Yeah. Okay. Go on ahead. I'll catch up." As they started up the stairs, they could see the vampire leaning against one of the apartment doors. He looked exhausted, ragged, and out of breath.

They made it to the eighth floor landing just as they heard one of the apartment doors on the seventh floor being broken open. Everyone froze, chanting within their heads, *"Don't do it, Raleigh. Don't do it."*

Then they heard the sound of a cat's hiss, followed by the snapping of jaws, and then silence. Another minute passed and Raleigh came jogging up the stairs, a spring in his steps and new life in his cheeks.

Chapter Nine:
   The Eighth Floor; The Queen of the Sea Songs

"You ate someone's cat!" Dory heard herself scream at Raleigh.

"Better than me eating you," he argued with indignation.

"I agree," Winston meekly added.

The young woman turned to Ghost in search of support, but he nodded his head. "I agree too. Better the cat than you."

Dory's stomach churned and she thought of a monster breaking into her apartment. She thought of Frank and fought back a whimper by letting out an angered screech. Tossing her arms in the air, Dory argued, "That was someone's pet. I bet the owners loved it and you've taken it away from them forever."

"I didn't kill it, just fed a little, I think. Anyway, it was just a cat," Raleigh muttered. He noticed how Dory lifted Frank and cuddled him protectively, "And it's not like I'd ever hurt your dog."

"You're all horrible. I'm so sick of this! Monsters!" Dory stormed off around the corner, stomping her feet a little as she walked, warning the three to keep a distance. She set down Frank, allowing him to run ahead until she lost track of his little furry body. Her temper tantrum noises caught the attention of one of the apartment residents. A young woman opened her door wide and stood watching Dory for a long minute. Dory paused when she felt eyes upon her.

The young woman waved Dory into her apartment. "You look tired. Do you need help? Need to borrow a phone?"

Dory glanced back at where she'd left the trio of monsters. She looked again at the girl with bouncy blonde hair and sharp cheekbones. She was her age, maybe a year or two younger. She wore a loose fitting blue sundress and sandals. Her smile was friendly, inviting, as if she were greeting an old school chum.

"You new to the building?" she asked. Dory realized how strange a normal conversation seemed to her.

With a nod Dory told her, "I just moved onto the first floor."

The other young woman whistled. "First floor. What are you doing all the way up here?"

"Off to see the Landlord," Dory explained with an exhausted sigh. "And discovering that this building is bigger than I thought."

The young woman's smile grew with understanding. "Don't I know it. It's like I have to ration my groceries just to make the trip up and down the stairs." She extended a hand and told her, "I'm Lorelei. I moved in here last year."

"Dory," she answered shaking her hand. "I think you're the first live person our age I've seen in this building."

Lorelei raised an eyebrow curiously at Dory. "Live person?"

Catching her mistake, Dory quickly restated, "You know, not on TV or in the brochure. Why do you live so far up?"

"Only vacancy at the time." She leaned in and whispered as if the walls had ears, "I have some of the weirdest neighbors. Really creepy sort. It's like living on Mockingbird Lane."

Dory laughed. "I know! You should see the lady in the apartment above me. She takes Crazy Cat Lady to a new level."

"Oh yeah!" Lorelei jokingly challenged. "My next door neighbor plays opera music on an organ at all hours of the night and he always wears a ski cap, even in summer."

"You thinking what I'm thinking?" Dory asked her.

"I prefer just not to think about it," Lorelei remarked. "Sometimes I swear this place is watching me . . . like it's haunted or something." She then waved Dory into her apartment, as if concerned they were being spied upon at that moment.

"Or something," Dory muttered, stealing one last look back at the place where she'd left her companions.

"This is fun," Lorelei exclaimed. "I never get to really talk to anyone about my neighbors. Come on in. You want a soda or something?"

Dory followed behind this new friend as they entered the apartment. The walls were painted a cheerful blue and the plush furniture was a grayish green. The curtains were white with wavy lines patterned across them. They were wide open to allow the sunlight to fall freely over the room. It was the brightest thing Dory had seen since she started her little adventure. She took a seat on one of the green easy chairs which surrounded the white wood coffee table. Atop the table sat a large shell, the kind that a person could blow into in order to make a trumpeting sound.

"That's a conch shell," Lorelei clarified when she saw Dory eye it curiously. She lifted it up to her lips and exhaled into the hole at one end. A mournful noise echoed throughout the apartment. "Neat, huh! Okay, soda. What kind do you like?" The blonde vanished into her kitchen, which was in a separate room unlike Dory's tiny apartment.

"Oh, whatever's fine," Dory answered, suddenly embarrassed and self-conscious. She knew she should have told the others where she was, but she also loved the thought of a new friend. A voice at the back of her brain reminded her that this friend would move away, leave her alone, and never call or write. Still, she sat and enjoyed the smile of someone who just wanted to gab. She'd spent so much time with the guys over the last twenty-four hours that she was beginning to worry about her own sanity.

Lorelei returned from the kitchen with two cans of clear soda and a plate of various snacks. "I never get to play hostess either so I'm sorta going all out. Is it too weird that I'm offering you food when we barely know each other?"

"Weirder things have happened to me," Dory told her as she accepted a piece of bread and cheese from the plate, thinking to herself. "Recently, I should add."

Her hostess squinted playfully and the expression of elation on her face grew. "Good, because I think we should be friends. It would be nice to know I have someone in the building to count on." Lorelei pointed at her television and added happily, "We can have movie nights and stuff like that."

Dory was surprised by Lorelei's eagerness, but found she liked the idea. "That sounds like fun. I can bring chips or something." She heard footsteps in the hallway and realized that the boys were approaching. She felt herself groan.

"What is it?" Lorelei asked with a worried expression pointed at the closed door.

"My—" Dory paused to think of the right word. At last, she settled on "friends." She moved at a slow pace to ready herself. "I better get going. They don't know where I am right now. Thanks for the soda," Dory said pointing to the unopened can. "Maybe we can do that movie night soon."

Lorelei shook her hand. "Psh! Why not start now? I'm sure your friends could come in too. Do they all like musicals?"

"I doubt it. They're all of the straight male persuasion," Dory said with a laugh, trying to imagine Raleigh keeping quiet through two hours men in tap shoes expressing their love for the heroine through song.

"Oh." Lorelei's tone turned dark. "Men. Men are coming to take you away from me." She stared down into her soda can, focusing on the blackness she could witness through the aluminum hole.

"Huh?" The word choice of the other young woman startled Dory.

Lorelei instantly perked up. "Oh, sorry. I'm babbling. Hey, before you go, do you want to hear a track off my album? I was in a garage band a couple of years back. We never went anywhere, but we were good. I never get to play it for anyone. Do you mind?"

A little taken aback, Dory told her, "No. That would be great. But maybe only one song. If I'm gone too long the guys will worry." She settled back against the chair, her body loosing tension as her brain spoke out harshly, *"You don't have time for this."*

"Of course, of course," Lorelei replied with a certain absent mindedness as she hopped over to her stereo. "We were called the Rocky Shores." She picked a CD case from a collection of albums and placed the disk into the player carefully. She pressed play and Dory found herself swaying a little to the music which came out.

It was a melodic alternative rock. Lorelei was obviously the soprano on lead vocals, singing of the sea and the beauty of the sky. The style was fast, yet beautiful with a heavy bass and a small amount of violin music complimenting the guitar riffs.

Over the beat, Dory almost thought she heard Raleigh shouting, but ignored it. She smiled at Lorelei to tell her silently how good the former band was. She looked around the apartment as if the décor somehow complimented the sounds. As her eyes scanned to the front door, she saw Ghost's face sticking in through the wood. He looked worried, yet embarrassed about poking his nose where it didn't belong.

"I'm okay," she mouthed to him and waved for him to go away before Lorelei saw him.

Instead, he entered the apartment and tried to talk to her over the music, not caring that the other young woman could see him. Over the thumping bass, the only thing Dory could hear him say was, "Winston" and "Not good".

She turned to Lorelei apologetically who was staring at Ghost with wide eyes. "Can you turn it down a little?" she requested. Lorelei reluctantly turned a knob and the music became a dull roar. With the volume lowered, Dory quickly told her hostess, "Sorry. This is one of my friends. He doesn't usually break and enter like this. Can you excuse us for just a second?"

Lorelei nodded, and then turned to face the window. She was humming along with her own song and seemed distracted by something outside.

"Now, what's not good?" Dory hissed at Ghost.

"Winston. He climbed out the . . . well, see!" Ghost pointed at the sill and there was Winston, balancing along the concrete ledge outside. His eyes were glazed over and his hands ran lightly over the side of the building, showing no signs of terror or danger.

"Holy hell!" Dory shouted, rushing to the window and sliding the pane upwards. She leaned out slightly and shouted, "Winston, what are you doing?"

"Raleigh wanted to go after him, but he can't go in the sunlight and I can't leave the building," Ghost explained. "It was weird. He was in the middle of saying something and then he went silent. Next thing we knew he'd broken into one of the apartments and climbed out."

Dory turned to Lorelei, who continued to hum and

stare at Winston on the ledge intently. "Can you turn that off and call 911?" Dory requested of her new friend.

Lorelei shook her head no. Between hums, she sing-songed, "Both my sisters left me to marry, grow old, and die. Men are just playthings. They forgot that." She then sang out over the CD, "Jump, my dear man. All of your wildest dreams are there; all you need to do is jump for them."

With a gasp, Dory realized, "You're doing this! Please, stop. He's not a threat. In fact, Winston's the most un-threatening guy I've ever met." She then turned back out the window. "Winston, listen to me! Don't jump!"

"Yes. Jump," Lorelei sang sweetly.

Winston began to edge a foot out over the precipice and Dory heard herself scream. She attempted to climb out onto the ledge to get him, but a banging against the front door of the apartment made her pause. Raleigh shoved himself against the door lock and ran in passed Ghost and Dory. The sunlight began to brown and burn his skin, but still he ran. He made it to the stereo which he instantly switched off. Then, he turned to the singing Lorelei and punched her squarely in the nose. She stumbled back and held her face with both hands. Her eyes welled with a mixture of shock and tears. Raleigh took the opportunity to collide his fist with her cheek. She fell to the floor, unconscious, her dress and hair splayed around her like waves.

The instant she was socked, Winston snapped out of his reverie. "Shit!" he shouted and pinned himself against the side of the building, "What the—Why am I out here? Oh, God. Help! Somebody help!"

Meanwhile, Raleigh was doing his own screaming at the pain of his seared flesh as the light filtered steadily through the window. Ghost pointed for him to hide behind the couch. "No sunlight back here," he told him.

As Raleigh dove for cover, Dory dealt with Winston. She edged herself against the sill and reached out her arm to him. "Take my hand. I'll help you in."

"Yeah, yeah," Winston muttered trying not to look down at the street below. "Your hand. Right. But what if I fall?"

Dory glanced down once, instantly feeling dizzy. For as small as the building seemed from the street, from the twelfth floor it was a giant reaching up to the sky. "I won't let you fall. Now come on."

"I think I'm going to be sick," Winston stated, turning a little green.

"Don't get sick. You might hit someone on the street and then they'd sue you," Ghost said rationally as he moved to the edge of the window. He wished he could hold onto Dory's feet. "This is ridiculous. The two live people are out on a ledge and the two dead people can't do anything to help. What's the point of being dead if you can't use it to help people every once in a while?"

Dory looked back at him as she moved a little further out onto the ledge, the wind rushing past her ears. "Help me coax him in. You can reason with him."

"Reason with him," Ghost repeated. "Okay, got it." His voice rang out of the window and caught on the wind in a haunting manner, "Wiiiiinston. Wiiiiinston." Ghost stopped and thought about what he had just done. "Hey, that was creepy."

"Great," Dory muttered sarcastically. "Practice later."

"Sorry." Ghost threw his voice again, trying to make it sound more soothing than scary. "Winston, come off the ledge, buddy. Take Dory's hand. Look at all those disgusting, unsanitary pigeon droppings. You don't want to live on the ledge, do you?"

"You don't want to die on a ledge, do you?!" Raleigh shouted from behind the couch.

"Raleigh!" Dory, Winston, and Ghost yelled in unison.

Dory added, "Not helping."

Winston felt his tense body begin to shake. "I'm going to fall!"

"Go wolf!" Ghost announced.

"WHAT?" the others said back with horror.

"You're claws can scrape through a lot of things, right? I bet you could grab the brick and pull yourself along the ledge back into the window," Ghost explained.

Winston protested, "No, no, no, no! I'm too panicked. I'll change completely! I'll kill Dory!"

"I won't let you," Ghost told him with confidence.

"Neither will I," shouted Raleigh from behind the couch.

"Oh, that's comforting," Winston moaned as he felt his weight begin to shift foreword. "Oh crap! Ohcrapohcrap."

Dory moved further down the ledge. "I'm coming to get you, but you have to meet me halfway." She tried to feel confident but her own fingers were trembling as they griped the window frame.

"I'll fall." The words came out quiet, yet still panicked. He looked at her with wild eyes as her own feet teetered on the concrete building. "You're going to fall!"

"Then use your claws. Climb over to me." Dory paused for a moment, tempted to look downward at the street below. Instead, she locked her gaze upon Winston. "Concentrate. You did it before in the apartment just a few minutes ago. You can do it again."

"I need Frank to lick me or something," he protested.

"No. No, you don't. Just concentrate." Dory stretched out her arm, attempting to reach his fingertips, which were scrapped and white as they dug into the wall. In that instant, she felt the breeze. She felt the wonder of the air against her face and the exhilaration of adrenalin from being so high up. A moment later the feeling was gone and she realized that she was about slip from the edge. One foot fell, dangling over the side and Dory scrambled to grab a hold of the window sill.

Ghost wanted to grab her, but his hands passed straight through. Dory screamed.

"What's going on?" Raleigh asked from behind the couch.

Winston's hands seemed to respond to Dory's cries of pain and terror. His fingers extended out, his nails became long and razor sharp. One fur covered claw punched into the brick building and gripped as best it could against the rough stone. The other claw grabbed for Dory, careful not to scratch her. The fur tickled her sweating palm. After a great deal of pulling, tugging, kicking, and clawing, the pair of them were back inside.

Sitting on the window sill, Dory threw her arms around Winston's neck. "Thank you." Winston responded with a series of puppy whimpers.

Sitting up, awoken by the screaming, Lorelei rolled her eyes. "Oh brother. Grow a pair, you over grown hound dog!" She then looked at Dory with concern. "Are you okay? You know, you didn't have to go out there to get him. I wouldn't have actually made him jump."

Winston replied with a further moan and moved slowly away from the window. Dory followed him without saying anything, as if afraid to meet the siren's gaze.

"Sirens suck! Let's get the heck out of here," Raleigh voted as he wrapped a throw blanket from the end of the couch around himself like a cloak.

Dory agreed and started to follow. Lorelei called out to her, "Dory, what about movie night?"

"I have to go." She dodged Lorelei's gaze. "And you tried to kill—" She glanced over at the werewolf and her heart felt a little twinge of protectiveness. "My friend."

"I'm sorry. I just wanted you to stay." Lorelei ran in front of Dory, blocking her exit. "Won't you please stay just a little longer?" Her eyes were wide with a mad fright, loneliness carving depressed lines in her face.

Dory had a mixed expression, somewhere between desperately wanting to stay, wanting to have frivolous girl-talk and watch ridiculously sappy films, and knowing she should be furiously storming out the door. "I better not." She muttered under her breath and forced her feet to take one more step forward.

"I thought we were going to be friends," Lorelei said, obviously hurt. Dory's own eyes stared up at the siren pityingly.

"Oh brother, come on, Dory," Raleigh groaned. "Don't listen to this crap. It smells like fish in her here."

Winston shakily whispered, "Please, Dory. Let's leave."

As if she didn't hear the two boys, Dory continued her conversation with Lorelei. "How can I trust you as a friend if you're going to be throwing my other friends off ledges?"

"I was just playing with him," Lorelei innocently replied.

"That was playing?!" Winston squeaked out, sounding like a pre-pubescent school boy.

"That was not playing," Dory clarified, trying to make her tone hard.

Lorelei waved her hands about. "Oh alright! If I swear upon my life that I'll never again try to harm another of your little boyfriends, then will you be my friend?"

"That seems reasonable," Dory responded, hope forming her voice, then glanced behind her as if she waited for the approval of the three males.

Ghost, Raleigh, and Winston nearly choked on their own tongues. Ghost was the first to speak. "Dory, what are you doing? Just because she swears it doesn't mean she can't be lying—"

Raleigh corrected him, "Actually, she can't. It's part of being an ancient Greek monster. If she swears something, she has to uphold it." His head rolled over to Dory, his voice instantly losing a clinical tone. "But still, Dory are you nuts!"

"Why?" Lorelei cooed, at last addressing the three men in the room. "Because she wants to have a friend who she can actually talk to, not one who is probably just out for something."

"We've been perfect gentlemen," Ghost defensively argued.

"Speak for yourself," Raleigh admitted. "Sorry, Dory, but I checked you out. You are somewhat hot and I am, after all, a vampire. I'm supposed to check people out so I can complement and seduce them. But that doesn't I mean was 'out' for whatever she's implying."

"Oh now," Lorelei warningly went on, "don't play coy you three. A werewolf, a vampire, and a ghost hanging around with a human. That can only mean you're after her flesh and blood. Even if you aren't now, when you get desperate enough, you will be."

Winston hung his head at this remark and Raleigh glared. Ghost seemed confused, unsure of why he'd want to hurt Dory in any way. He was not a half anything or need blood to survive.

She was unrelenting in her accusations. "What makes you think that she's any safer with the three of you than she would be hanging around with me? Face it, boys, you might as well leave her here." The words came out in a hypnotizing song.

Raleigh scoffed, "Ghost and vampire, remember. Your trick doesn't work on us. Come on, Dory. This is getting stupid." He reached for her arm, but she shrugged him away.

"I think I want to stay," Dory said a little dazed.

"Yes," Lorelei proclaimed. "Yes! Yes! You want to

stay."

"No!" Ghost yelled back. "Dory is coming with us."

"No! She's my new friend and I'm keeping her!" Lorelei practically screamed. She stomped her foot like an angry child, then added with a pout, "Dory, don't you want to stay and be my friend?"

"Say no, Dory," Raleigh commanded.

Dory hesitated. Lorelei's healthy tan and gracious smile were so much more welcoming than the three guys with their pallor, their fur, and their transparent skin. The appearance of the siren transported her memory to days at school when she still had friends living close by. Thoughts of long talks about homework and crushes mixed with the smell of French fries and nail polish created a longing in her heart. She looked back and forth between the three and the girl, wondering which she really wanted to choose.

Winston threw his hands in the air. "She did just try to kill me, after all! Are you even thinking about that part?"

Ghost stepped up to Dory. He set a cold hand on her shoulder. She still felt no actual weight from the appendage, but the cool feeling that stretched from her shoulder to the rest of her body was oddly comforting, as if Ghost really was touching her. With his silver eyes searching out her brown ones, he asked her, "Do you really want to stay here for a little while? What about the Landlord? Don't you want to get your lease fixed?"

"I can get it fixed anytime," she argued with determination. "We were going to watch a movie."

"That's right! Maybe *Grease*," Lorelei suggested with temptation in her tone. "And we'll talk about our days and complain about past relationships. In my almost four thousand years, I've been with all kinds. I could tell you some really out-there stories about the guys I've dated."

Dory turned to her with excitement in her eyes. "Oh, I bet none of them compare to my college boyfriend. He was certifiable! I mean that literally. Men in white coats came to take him away."

Hovering over Dory's other shoulder, Raleigh growled, "She's luring you, trying to keep you here for her own purposes. Fight it, Dory!"

Lorelei cooed, "Are you going to let these guys tell you what to do? Come on, you survived dating a lunatic and you're going to take advice from a vampire? I should tell you about when I was living in Italy at the turn of the century and one of my sisters actually got an inventor to design a plane just in her honor—"

Dory laughed, "Really?"

"Dory! Focus!" Ghost snapped at her. She looked back at him. Raleigh and Winston stood behind him with conflicted expressions. Ghost sternly asked her, "What about Frank?"

"Frank?" At first the name sounded distant. The image of a little dog with wiry golden fur and short, floppy ears entered her mind's eye. The memory wagged his tail at her. "Frank!" She looked at Ghost mournfully and admitted, "I forgot about him."

"He's out in the hallway still. I'm sure he'll forgive you, but we have to find him first," Winston stated, keeping a safe distance from the siren.

Lorelei hissed, "Stay with me!"

Turning to her apologetically, Dory told her with sadness, "I can't. I have to go. But I can come back. I can be your friend without you having to kill my other friends or play tricks on my mind."

"You won't come back." Lorelei wailed, tears falling from her eyes, "I know it. I know it."

Dory placed her hands on her hips. "Oh, for Pete's sake. Four thousand years old and you act this way? Seriously?" She sighed before adding, "You'll see. I'll be back and I'll bring a whole stack of girl bonding movies with me and nail polish."

Lorelei stopped her weeping. "Really?" she quietly asked, almost shyly.

"I promise," Dory put in with honesty. "Just no more trying to sing Winston off the side of the building, okay."

"Yeah!" Winston added with a sneer.

"You. Don't talk," Dory said to the werewolf, and then turned back to Lorelei. "What you do say? Friends?"

She held out a hand to the siren who took it almost reluctantly. "Friends," she muttered. "But if you don't come to see me, mark my words, I will hunt you down and make you sorry."

"Consider your words marked," Dory said. She felt Raleigh and Winston each grab one of her arms and pull her out of the apartment. Ghost walked behind acting as a shield between Lorelei and Dory. They glared at one another, but Ghost noticed something else in the siren's eyes. It was concern for her new friend.

When the group was back in the hall with a door safely barricading them from the siren, Raleigh released Dory and angrily stated, "You should have let me kill her."

"Why? Maybe I could use a friend," Dory countered as they headed for the next staircase.

"You're not seriously going back in there?" Winston gasped.

"I promised," Dory said smugly, "and maybe I need a little boy bashing every now and again. You guys are exhausting." She paused to squeeze Winston's arm, then gave Raleigh a half hug, and smiled gratefully at Ghost. "Thanks for looking out for me though. Either way you look at it, I sort of need you guys too."

"Damn straight you do," Raleigh proudly told her.

"Don't get cocky," Ghost told the vampire, while winking at Dory. "We're almost there. Next stop, ninth floor."

"With no more surprises, I hope," Dory added with an exhausted expression. "I don't know how much more of this I can take."

As they rounded the corner of the stairs and neared the next floor, Ghost wondered aloud, "Did you really have a boyfriend who was certifiably nuts?"

"Yep," Dory said with a shrug of her shoulders. "He believed that the school faculty were aliens out to get him. He attacked one of our professors with a pen and they hauled him away. At the time, I thought he was out of his mind, but after everything thing that's happened, maybe he's the first sane person I've ever really known." She thought again over her own words and further said, "Wow, that's sad. What would he say of my life now? 'Ghosts and vampires and werewolves . . . oh crap'."

Chapter Ten:
    The Ninth Floor; The Deadly Hallway

The ninth floor was shrouded in a heavy fog. It crept along the floor in waves. Every once in a great while, a clear spot would open and the floor would become visible. The upwards staircase was once again at the opposite end of the hallway, the fog rolling down each step in billows of gray and white.

"Hey, Lon Chaney Jr., why don't you live on this floor?" Raleigh asked Winston with a teasing jab to the arm.

Winston protested, "This place gives me the creeps."

"Every place gives you the creeps," Raleigh muttered, upset that no one laughed at his joke. He then noticed Winston's hanging head. "Sorry. I didn't mean that. You've been really brave lately, when it comes down to it."

"I have?" Winston asked with a quiver of his shoulders.

"If I'd have been hanging off that ledge . . . and still alive, I would have wet myself," Ghost admitted, and then glanced at Dory with a slight red in his translucent cheeks. "Metaphorically, I mean. I wouldn't have literally wet myself—"

"We got it, let it go," Raleigh told him.

Dory added, "Winston, you were really impressive back there. Very calm under pressure." Her fingers folded within her palm to feel where the bricks had scraped her skin.

"Yeah?" Winston thought back upon his moment of

peril and confirmed, "Yeah. I was, wasn't I?"

"You bet—" Raleigh's words tapered off as he noticed a golden fuzz ball on the floor as the fog temporarily cleared. A second later, the fog covered the form once again. He looked worriedly at Dory.

"What is it?" she asked inquisitively.

Raleigh thought about how heartbroken the young woman would be if her dog were dead. He didn't want her to be the one to find out first. If Frank was dead he'd rather tell her, let her be prepared before seeing her little puppy lying on the fog covered hallway. "I'm not sure. Stay back here. Winston, Ghost, you stay with her."

Winston smelled Frank, the scent finally rising over the musty smell of the mist, and knew what was going on. He set an arm across Dory's front and told her, "Just in case."

"In case of what?" she wanted to know. "Is something going to jump out of the fog and get us? What's going on?"

"Just stay there," Raleigh insisted. He moved slowly towards the spot where he'd seen Frank, afraid that quick movements would stir the fog and reveal the little dog. He leaned down carefully, feeling through the fog. He felt an ear then moved his hand down to the dog's belly. It moved up and down at a steady pace. Raleigh breathed a sigh of relief. "It's Frank. He's asleep."

Winston released Dory who rushed to the spot in the fog. She lifted up her little dog and pet him behind the ear. "You goofball. Okay, wake up." She shook him a little. "Frank? Frank? Wake up. Want to go for a walk? Want a treat? How about a ride in the car?" Her voice reached a frightened squeak by the last suggestion. A fluttery feeling encased her heart.

Nothing worked. The puppy continued to snooze, wiggling every now and again as he dreamed of chasing small woodland creatures. "He won't wake up," Dory said, not realizing that she, herself was yawning. She slid down the side of the wall into a sitting position. Laying Frank across her lap, she propped up her arm with one hand.

Winston rubbed his eyes as he staggered forward towards them. "I'm not surprised. It's been a long day. I'm pretty beat myself." He sat down alongside sprawling across the middle of the floor.

"What's with you two?" Ghost asked. The fog rolled through his legs as he walked towards them. "Come on, we're almost there. We can sleep after we talk to the Landlord."

"I just need to rest my feet for a minute," Dory muttered as her head began to bob back and forth in an attempt to say awake.

Ghost crouched down in front of her. The young woman's eyelids fluttered. "Are you just resting your eyes too?"

"Mmm hmmm," she murmured, her eyelashes batting frantically to stay open.

Raleigh pointed at Winston, "Check out Sleeping Beauty." Winston lay sprawled amongst the fog, his arms and legs spread out like he was making a snow angel. A noise like a lawnmower echoed from deep within the werewolf and came out through his nose and mouth.

Ghost attempted to move Dory, but his hand went straight through. "Something's not right," he said as she laid her head down and succumbed to sleep.

"What do we do?" Raleigh asked, taking his own turn at shaking both Winston and Dory, yet neither stirred.

Jumping back to his feet, Ghost began to poke his head into each apartment door, not caring whose privacy he was invading. In each flat, he found more people passed out, resting peacefully sprawled on couches and floors. "They're all asleep." He looked down at the floor, the smoke curling around the people, not disturbing them in the least. "I think it's the fog. We need to get them out of the fog."

"I could carry Dory, but I don't think I can handle wolfy over there," Raleigh said jabbing an annoyed finger in Winston's direction. "And we can't leave him here."

"I thought vampires were supposed to be super strong," Ghost criticized.

"We're abnormally strong, not comic book mutants," Raleigh corrected.

"What about the siren?" Ghost asked after a moment's thought, "If she could control Winston to throw himself off a building, couldn't she get him to walk upstairs."

"Can we trust her?" Raleigh wanted to know.

"Do we have a choice?" Ghost countered.

They ran back downstairs and Raleigh pounded a fist on the Siren's door. "Get out here, you old harpy!"

Ghost looked ready to kill the vampire. "Nice. You should really go into motivational speaking." He called tentatively into the door, "Miss Siren? Um, Lorelei. We need help. Dory's in trouble and we—"

The door flew open and the siren faced them with a frown. She curtly told him, "Talk fast, earthbound spirit."

"The fog on the next floor knocked out Dory and Winston. We can move Dory, but Winston's another story." Ghost told her this as meekly, yet panicked as he could.

"And why should I help that fur ball wannabe?" Lorelei asked while shining the backs of her manicured nails on her dress.

Raleigh impatiently answered with, "To do a good deed and earn Karma points. Come on, lady. We need your help."

Ghost thought through his next words logically before speaking. "Because if you leave Winston there to waste away in a dream state, do you think Dory will ever want to have a movie night with you?"

The siren shifted her weight, thinking over the possibilities in her head. At last she sighed. "Oh, all right! But this is the only time I'll help. Next time, you're on your own."

They returned to the ninth floor. The fog had nearly hidden Dory and Winston beneath it. Lorelei let out another long sigh at the sight. "Really? I can't believe you were all dumb enough to get caught in such a trap."

"Just help us," Ghost pleaded.

Raleigh lifted Dory into his arms. Frank lay curled up in her lap and he carried the two of them over to the stairs leading to the tenth floor. Even with his advanced strength, he grunted as he balanced the two to them, Dory's hair ticking his nose. As he passed Ghost, he whispered, "Watch her. If she tries anything funny, call me back down."

Ghost nodded and hovered over the siren. Lorelei flipped her hair at him. "Oh for gods' sake. Back off, you Dickens reject. I won't hurt your slobbering, disgusting buddy."

She tilted her head back and forth while rotating her shoulders, as if the simple exercise would make her voice louder. Her bottom jaw dropped and a long, lovely note echoed from within her. She hummed, then sang. The lyrics were all about long walks, strong steps, and moving forward. Despite the obvious metaphors, Winston's unconscious body rose up from the floor. His eyes remained shut tight, but his legs carried him through the hallway like a sleepwalking sufferer. His arms hung limply at his sides and his head fell backwards so his snores trumpeted like a bullhorn.

Lorelei continued to sing as the sleeping werewolf tripped up each step. She followed behind him with Ghost close behind her. When they reached the tenth floor, she instantly quieted and Winston collapsed. His head slammed down, jarring him awake.

Sitting bolt upright, Winston's eyes flew upon. "What? What happened?" He gazed around in daze and scrambled to his feet to up from the filthy floor. Pointing at Lorelei, he fitfully asked, "Why is she here?" His finger then traveled to Dory who was slowly waking from her own sleep. "What happened to Dory?"

The girl blinked as her head pivoted back and forth. Ghost filled them in on the recent events. "Lorelei, that was an incredibly decent thing to do," Dory told the siren with praise.

Lorelei had her arms crossed over her chest and said with attitude, "Look at me, I saved Jim Jim the dog faced boy. Goody. Can I go home now?"

Dory smiled at her. "Yes. Thank you. So, girly movie night next week?"

Lorelei's shoulder's tilted back and she bobbed her head with the same attitude. "Oh, you bet your boots. And just because I had to rescue the mongrel, you're bringing chips and salsa!"

"See you then," Dory told her with appreciation.

As they watched the siren walk away back down the stairs, Raleigh commented, "I have to say, present company included, that you pick the weirdest friends, Dory."

"Oh no. Don't you make this my fault," Dory cautioned. "I wasn't looking for friends. I just wanted to talk to the Landlord. You guys found me."

"Speaking of—" Winston chimed in pointed at a bright green door, "We're here."

Chapter Eleven:
    The Tenth Floor; The Knocker of the Door

The door seemed to glow in the dark hallway. Hanging on the front of the door was a brass face with a long handle hanging below its chin. The face's eyes were closed and the jaw shut tightly as if the model for the face had suffered from painful dental work before the knocker was molded.

"What does this remind me of?" Ghost asked, standing nose to nose with the wrinkled brass face.

Dory also inspected the knocker on the heavy door. "It looks like the character from the Dickens' novel."

Raleigh rubbed his chin and asked, "The Artful Dodger." The vampire had paled greatly, his fingers quivering. His heroics in the siren's apartment had worn down the nutrition the cat's blood had provided him. Dory knew that hunger would get the better of him soon despite his casual smile. He was careful to stay as far to one side of the hallway as possible, pressing his shoulder into the wall as if it would keep him from attacking his friends.

"Literature is not your strong suit, is it," Winston groaned not noticing Raleigh's weakened state. "She's talking about Jacob Marley, the first ghost in 'A Christmas Carol'."

"A ghost," Ghost repeated with interest. "I should read that book."

"I'm sure you did when you were alive," Dory pointed out. "Or at least saw one of the many movie versions. So? Who's going to knock?" She glanced at each of the men who each pretended to be interested in their shoes. "Wusses," she accused and stepped through Ghost to lift the heavy brass handle. She dropped the knocker three times. The group waited.

The sound of metal rubbing against metal made Dory jump. She almost fell backwards through Ghost who attempted to catch her, only for his hands to pass into her shoulders. The eyes of the knocker popped open and the coppery expression glared at the four people.

"Do you have an appointment?" the knocker asked them. His voice vibrated like a base amplifier. He blinked at them creating the clanging sound of the brass moving.

"How could we get an appointment?" Raleigh demanded to know, flashing his fangs wearily. "We can't even call up here."

"It's just a standard question," the Marley knocker replied. "No need to get huffy, young man." The knocker then narrowed its eyes at Raleigh. "I beg your pardon. You're a vampire, are you not?"

Raleigh leaned against the wall looking a little like a James Dean impersonator. "Yeah. So."

"Hmm," the knocker said aloud. He seemed to want them to notice his deep, obvious pondering. At last, he stated, "And a werewolf, correct? And a ghost. What an unusual parade which has appeared at the Landlord's door." Scanning his eyes over Dory, he added, "And what are you, young lady?"

"Human," she told the knocker who was instantly disappointed.

"Oh. Well, I suppose the Landlord will still want to see you since you came with this lot. Let me try to announce you." With that, the face went perfectly still, looking again as a brass figure head should, motionless and lifeless.

"I think I preferred the spider," Winston murmured. Dory could see how faint the wolf was and wondered how a talking piece of metal could unnerve a grown man so.

Moving to stand beside him, Dory told Winston, "He's announcing us, right?"

"Right." Winston glanced at her sideways as she stood shoulder to shoulder with him.

"This will all be over soon. Nothing to worry about, okay." Dory rubbed a hand against his arm, similar to how a parent would comfort a frightened child after a nightmare as the door of the apartment opened on its own. "Ready with your question for him?"

"Yes. I'm ready," Winston said with renewed determination. The four of them entered the flat silently.

The Landlord's home seem to stretch for miles in either direction. For a moment, Dory wanted to point out the impossibility of such a large apartment existing in such a narrow building, but remembered where she was and bit her tongue. The four of them hooked arms as they walked into the open sitting area at the center of the apartment.

Everything had been done up in green. The textured wallpaper looked expensive with a Victorian paisley pattern adding a touch of flare. The floors were wood, well-polished and cared for. The lights were held in green crystal and a chandelier was hung from the main sitting room with emeralds hanging down from the edges of the light bulbs. A green linoleum table had been placed upon a floral print rug. Four matching chairs with sea foam green cushions awaited the travelers. Two tall wardrobes were positioned on the eastern and western walls of the room.

The Marley knocker's voice resounded overhead as if he were talking in a loudspeaker. "Refreshments are in the cupboards to the left, a change of clothes are available in the cupboard on the right," the knocker explained. "Help yourselves to anything."

"We really just want to see the Landlord and be on our way," Dory explained despite the weakness she felt and the gnawing pang in her stomach.

Winston and Raleigh had already opened the cupboard of the left. A cup of red liquid awaited the vampire and an uncooked steak was laid out on a plate for the werewolf. Raleigh drank greedily, a little bit of red dribbling down the corner of his mouth. His muscles relaxed and he collapsed into a chair with a contented sigh.

"You won't be able to see the Landlord today," knocker explained, "but first thing tomorrow, you will each be given a chance to have an individual audience."

"Individual," Winston stammered, a piece of meat hanging from his bottom jaw.

"The Landlord will only see one of you at a time," the knocker restated.

"Why tomorrow?" Ghost asked

"The Landlord has business to attend to tonight. Rooms will be provided for you down the east hallway. Please go nowhere near the west hallway until tomorrow morning when I announce you. If you disturb the Landlord you will face a most terrible punishment." The Marley knocker sounded very rehearsed, yet professional.

With a sigh, Dory gave in. She checked the refreshment cupboard. A chicken salad and root beer awaited her alongside a dish of kibble for Frank. She sat at the table with Raleigh and Winston, trying not to be disgusted by their meals. Ghost sat with them, even though he couldn't eat or rest.

After they were full, they checked the second cupboard. Clothing was hung up for people of all shapes and sizes, all of it green. "What's wrong with the clothes we have on?" Raleigh asked with defense for his expensive wardrobe.

"We've been wearing them for two days straight," Dory pointed out.

As if to check the girl's logic, Winston held up his arm

and sniffed at the pit. "Phew!" He gasped, "I smell like I've been rolling in garbage."

Raleigh chose the most stylish of the apparel, a pair of designer slacks which were such a dark shade of green that they appeared black upon first glance. He also found a soft green button up shirt and a forest green vest. Satisfied, he traveled down the hall to pick a room. Winston found a pair of khaki green cotton pants, like the sort soldiers wore. He chose a light green collared shirt which seemed to Dory to be no different than his yellow polo. Then, Winston was off to find a room of his own.

Ghost waited with Dory while she picked out something suitable to wear. She kept holding up shirts, skirts, and pants in front of herself to check for sizes and styles. Mournfully thinking of her own clothes resting still in cardboard boxes downstairs, Dory felt discouraged at trying to find an outfit. Frank curled up on a fallen jacket.

At last, she turned to Ghost, holding up a pair of jeans with green stitching and a jade colored V-neck top. "Okay, I know you're a guy, but what do you think?"

He nodded. "Nice." His eyes cast down to where Frank was asleep.

Dory, defeated, hung the clothes back into the wardrobe. "But . . ."

"I didn't say but," he defensively replied.

"There was a but in there. You didn't have to say it," she explained with a laugh.

Ghost leaned forward in his chair and sighed. "Okay. But don't you think you ought to dress more professional? You're trying to convince this man to rearrange a contract. Do you really want to do that in jeans?"

"You'll be in jeans," she replied.

"I don't have a choice. I died in these clothes," Ghost told her. "I can't ever wear anything else."

Dory raised her eyebrows at him. "Really? What if you

had died while naked?"

Ghost smirked at her playfully. "Well, then our first meeting would have been a tad embarrassing." He glanced down at his tee-shirt. "Maybe I died on my way to a concert."

Offering him a sympathetic expression, Dory tried to change the subject. "So, what do you think I should wear?"

He smiled sheepishly. "I don't know. Interview clothes."

Nodding and repeating back at him, "Interview clothes, huh," Dory practically climbed into the wardrobe. She dug around, pushing hangers this way and that until she produced a bundle of emerald green. "Okay, found something." She had a happy glint in her eye.

"Oh?" Ghost stood up and tried to inspect the fabric in her hands.

"I'll put it on tomorrow and you can see then," she told him. She started down the hallway and Frank instantly followed.

Ghost trailed after them, his hands stuffed into his pockets. Dory picked the third door down, pushing it open so Frank could run into the green room before her. The furniture was plush and gaudy, a soft Victorian twin bed was centered on a green rug just to the left of the bathroom door. "I need to sleep," she said feeling relief at seeing a bed.

"Do you want me to sit with you until you doze off?" Ghost asked glancing into the room at the distasteful furniture.

She sighed. A part of her wanted to say yes, to have the familiar face there near her bed as she started to drift. To know he could wake her if there was danger and that she could give him a little company during his restlessness was a nice thought, making her feel like she had a routine back to her life. Yet, she answered, "Good night, Ghost."

"Good night, Dory." He smiled at her one last time as she shut her door. Ghost chose another door and stepped through without opening it first. This room had no bed. Instead there was a chair and a folding table with a deck of cards. Whenever he was corporal, Ghost played solitaire. He thought about his afterlife and the wondered what kind of life he must have led.

His mind made lists as if he were a detective in a mystery novel, taking the assumptions his new friends into consideration. He was smart, but liked rock music, assuming the shirt he had died in was his, not something he'd borrowed from someone else. He remembered confusion and cold before he died so obviously whatever happened to him had been unexpected. And, if Raleigh was right, he had never had his heart broken. He considered these things, trying to imagine his existence in the living world until he heard the others stir a few hours after sunrise.

Chapter Twelve:
The Tenth Floor; The Wonderful Home of the Landlord

Dory came out into the hallway last with Frank hopping along her heels excited for a new day. The other three were already at the green linoleum table with another cup for Raleigh and a plate of eggs and pork for Winston. Ghost was watching them eat while they made light conversation. They all looked up as she entered, first focusing upon her usual ruby red sneakers.

The dress had a classic neckline, high and straight across, without sleeves. The bodice led down to a long waist that spread outward into a full, knee length skirt with a petticoat barely visible beneath. She resembled a character from a 1960s film, save for the shoes which should have clashed with the rich, green fabric. The dress had deep pockets hidden within the folds of material. As if it would bring her luck, Dory had kept the silver key in her left pocket. She placed the folded up lease in her right pocket, checking for it every few minutes. She had showered and brushed out her hair, giving her a refreshed glow.

She did not realize how different she looked.

Winston opened his mouth and a piece of bacon fell out. Raleigh instantly jumped up to pull out her chair for her. Ghost was smiling, but said nothing. When Dory gave him a questioning look as she sat down, he matched it.

"What?" she asked him.

The smile remained on his face and he answered, "What?"

Raleigh ignored the less than witty conversation and told Dory, "What my two comrades aren't articulate enough to say is that you look beautiful."

She blushed and meekly replied, "Um . . . thanks." Even guys she'd dated never told her she was beautiful or looked at her the way the three men were staring at that moment. Wanting to avoid her own embarrassment, almost wishing she hadn't chose the silly dress, Dory crossed her arms over her chest as she leaned back in her chair. She turned to rise again in order to retrieve breakfast, but Winston scrambled to his feet.

"I'll get it!" He ran to the cupboard and found a bowl of cereal waiting for Dory there. "Really?" he then asked, holding out the cereal to her.

"That looks like something I would eat, yes," Dory told him, taking the bowl from his hands. "Thanks."

As they finished eating, the Marley knocker's voice brought them out of a friendly reverie. "The Landlord will see you now."

"All of us?" Winston spoke with undeniable hope.

"No, one at a time," the voice answered, obviously having no qualms with dashing the werewolf's hopes. "First, the ghost. Follow the hallway to the office door and enter."

Glancing at his friends, Ghost rose and started down the hallway. "I'll come back and tell you all about it before you have to go in," he promised Winston as he left. He reached to the office door and gave his friends one last look. They seemed so far away after he had only traveled a few feet.

Ghost, feeling solid enough to at least touch objects, knocked. After a minute with no answer, he simple pushed open the door and entered. It closed behind him automatically. The office of the Landlord was bathed in green. Not only was the furniture, carpet, floor, and ceiling a lovely forest tint, the bulb in the lamp left the room in an eerie green glow. All four walls were lined with oak bookcases. The desk was made of oak painted green and the top was a cool green marble. There were no papers or pens or any of the usual office supplies cluttering the top. A jade colored green leather chair was faced backwards at the wide desk, the high back hiding who ever sat within it.

Ghost nervously waited for the chair to turn. He wasn't sure what to expect. He was almost fearful of the chair to swivel and reveal its owner.

The leather chair twisted and the occupant smiled at him sweetly with pouting lips. It was a woman, gorgeous in every way from her shapely silhouette to her delicate facial features. Her skin was a perfect tan hue and her eyes were the brightest of greens. The only unusual part of her was a pair of giant bat wings folded between her and the chair back. She wore a scandalously low cut, sleeveless dress made of a wispy green silk. She leaned forward to rest her elbows on the desk top and set her toned chin on the backs of her entwined fingers. Her dress slipped down a little further and Ghost tried to keep his eyes upon her face.

"And how can I help you?" she asked. Her voice was low and smooth like the vamp from an old mystery film.

"Well, I'm a ghost—" he started to say.

She made a noise like she had just eaten something delicious. "I can see that, handsome."

"Um, well . . . yeah . . . well," Ghost stumbled and tried to concentrate on the ceiling, "I was wondering about where I could haunt in the building because I'm not having any luck on my floor."

"Oh," she purred.

"No one is afraid of me," he further explained, sounding pitiful.

She giggled, "Oh, I wouldn't say that. Look at me; I'm trembling."

He continued to stare upwards and said with confusion, "I haven't even tried to scare you."

She sighed and relaxed her posture slightly, "Yes, you are a sad case."

Ghost dropped his gaze to hers hopefully. "So, you'll help me?"

"Not so fast, gorgeous," she informed him as she leaned back in the chair. "You have a floor that you belong on. I can't have you just frightening all of my tenants, now can I?"

"No, I guess not," he muttered with disappointment.

"I suppose we could come to an . . . arrangement," she suggested, leaning forward once again and letting her wings spread out a little.

Instantly, Ghost's instincts kicked in. "What kind of arrangement?" he asked her warily.

"I have a little situation with one of the upstairs neighbors. If you can rid my building of her, you can have free reign to haunt wherever you would like." She smiled at him again, this time her lips parting slightly and blowing him a kiss.

Logic overtook Ghost's shyness. "Why can't you just get rid of her yourself? You own the building, don't you?"

"Alas, this particular resident is . . . shall we say powerful. She lives on the thirteenth floor. If you could kick her out for me, then our deal will be cemented." She wiggled her eyebrows at him. "So?"

It was Ghost's turn to sigh. He thought about his long existence, his constant wanderings with so few people paying attention to him. Eventually, Dory would return to her old apartment building, Winston would vanish back into his home, and Raleigh would go back to whatever activities a vampire did to keep themselves occupied. He could not handle years of standing alone in that hallway again, watching people moving in and out of their homes, taking their lives for granted.

At last, he answered, "Alright. I'll do it."

"Should we kiss to seal the deal?" she said to him smoothly.

He almost laughed at this final attempt of the winged woman to get him to come nearer. "No. Thanks."

"Very well," she said with disappointment, "Exit through the side door if you would."

Ghost turned to the right. Where a bookcase had been was now a plain brown door. He left through it, curious about where he would end up.

Meanwhile, back in the waiting room, the Marley knocker called out, "Next, the vampire. Follow the hallway down to the office door and enter."

"Wait, where's Ghost?" Dory called upward. "He hasn't come back yet."

Winston rocked a little in his seat and gave Raleigh a panicked stare. "Yeah. What have you done with him?"

"Nothing," the knocker simply answered. "Now, if the vampire would please follow the hallway down to the office door and enter."

Raleigh shook his head. "There's nothing I hate more than orders from a disembodied voice." Rising from his chair and starting down the hallway, he called back to Winston and Dory, "See you on the other side, I hope."

Raleigh didn't bother to knock before entering. The room appeared to be empty. He acknowledged that the desk chair was backwards, but did not wonder about it being occupied. Raleigh was tempted to mess with objects on the shelves and to riffle through the Landlord's book collection. Just then the chair at the desk pivoted around to face him. Sitting there, hunched over as if it were perfectly natural, sat a horrific Minotaur. His back stayed up straight, looking to be at least seven feet in height. His face was a mash-up of bull and human from the horns poking from his fur covered head to his broad human shoulders leading down to his muscular arms.

It took all of the vampire's will power to keep him from backing away in surprise. "You're the Landlord?"

He snorted through his bull nose, steaming the gold ring hanging from his nostrils. "What?" he barked at Raleigh. "Get on with it!"

"On with what?" Raleigh asked, hoping that the monster's burly arms would stay at his sides. Even with his powers, he could never fight off a monster three times his size with mythological strength. He could already picture what an angry Minotaur could do to him. Just a crack from the wide hands could dislocate Raleigh's neck from his shoulders, another way to destroy a vampire.

"Why are you here, wasting my time?" the deep voice bellowed as the Minotaur narrowed his beady red eyes.

"I—" Raleigh could suddenly relate better to Winston, feeling his body shake with worry.

"Are you going to answer or can I just break your scrawny body? Your bones would make good toothpicks!" The Minotaur drooled a little, and then wiped his mouth uncouthly on the back of his hand.

The fear turned to an adrenaline punch of anger. "I just need a way to keep the sunlight out of my apartment, you moron!" Raleigh heard himself yell then instantly regretted his harsh words.

The Landlord settled against his chair, his horns only a foot from the low ceiling. "That's a fairly realistic request, but—"

"But?" Raleigh hated that word.

"But to do that right would involve a great deal of reconstruction to the apartment, meaning that after you move out I'll have to re-do it all. So I'm going to need something from you," the Minotaur explained, tapping his hoof on the floor so it echoed across the wood floor.

"I'll pay for the construction," Raleigh volunteered.

"No." The Landlord pointed upwards. "Help me get rid of the Obnoxious Neighbor on the thirteenth floor and I will have any changes you need made to your apartment."

"You're a huge, scary Greek beast. Can't you just eat her or something?" Raleigh could hear Dory in his head complaining about how insensitive and rude he was being, but didn't care.

The Minotaur landlord stopped tapping his hoof. "I am a business man, Mr. Vampire; I do not go around eating my residents." He then snorted at the young man and added, "Besides, are you really going argue with me?"

Raleigh smacked his lips as he thought. "No. No, I guess not. Okay, I'll get rid of your damn obnoxious lady. How do I get out of here?"

The door against the side wall appeared again, popping through the book shelves like a secret passage. Raleigh walked out of the door, but grumbled to himself all the way out of room.

Winston and Dory were left in the waiting room alone. She offered him a million reassuring smiles, but Winston only chewed at his fingernails. After what felt like hours of silence, he finally asked, "I don't see why we can't go in together."

Dory just nodded at him, not certain if she could put together an answer for him based around the sketchy details she knew about the Landlord.

"Where are the others?" he asked, his breath coming out in slow, heavy sighs, "Why haven't Raleigh and Ghost come back out?"

"I don't know," Dory quietly answered, craning her neck to see the door at the end of hallway.

As if the Marley knocker had heard them, it

announced, "Werewolf, the Landlord will see you now. Follow the hallway to the office door and enter."

Looking anxiously at Dory in search of one final reassuring smile, Winston straightened his polo shirt and started down the hall. He entered the same door he had seen Raleigh and Ghost go through. The room left Winston with an even greater feeling of horror. The green light made him think of a childhood haunted house and the squeak in the desk chair as it turned left him trembling. The chair, however, was occupied by a skeleton on fire. The fire did not seem to affect the desk or the chair. The thick scent of smoke was nowhere to be found. The room still smelled of musty books with the slight hint of oil like a car was somewhere in the room leaking transmission fluid.

The skeleton landlord stared at Winston with empty sockets being licked by flames. The bottom jaw moved stiffly up and down as it addressed him. "And what can I do for you, Werewolf?"

Winston stammered with fear yet managed to ask, "Sssss . . . should I get a fire essssss . . . extinguisher?"

"Why? I'm perfectly toasty and comfortable," the Landlord answered with humor in his voice. "Again, why are you here?"

Winston leaned on one of the bookshelves for support. His legs had turned to Jell-O beneath him and he could feel an anxiety attack threatening to destroy his doggedness. "I—I—I—"

The skeleton's hands clasped in front of him and the skull tilted back in annoyance. "Oh, get on with it!"

"I want better chains in my apartment for when I change!"

"For when you turn into a wolf?" the Landlord clarified.

Winston nodded, paying close attention to the skeleton's rib cage, trying to imagine he was staring into a barbeque grate with smoldering ashes and not the bones of a former human being.

The Landlord said, "Very well, but you must do something for me. Get rid of the Obnoxious Neighbor on the thirteenth floor."

"You mean, talk to her?" Winston swallowed hard at the idea. "You want me to confront her."

"If you want me to help you, then you must do this for me," the skeleton restated, "or would you rather have no precaution over your transformations? If that's the case, then good luck to you."

He tried to imagine not being able to stop himself from attacking. He cringed inward at the thought of his furniture being shredded by his maniac alter ego; the plastic covers being torn off and ending their protection over his sofa and chairs. His heartbeat sped up and the edges of the room seemed to be getting dark. "I'll do it!" Winston managed to spit out before he collapsed on the floor.

As he passed out he heard the terrifying landlord say, "Oh, good grief."

The thud of the wide man falling onto the floor traveled down the hallways. Dory jumped in her seat at the sound. "What was that?" the young woman still in the waiting room asked.

Instead of an answer, Dory heard the door knocker's voice echo, "The Landlord will see you now. Follow the hallway to the office door and enter."

"I heard you the first three times," Dory muttered under her breath. She scooped up Frank and stepped down the long corridor. She closed the door behind her as she entered the office. When the chair at the desk swiveled around, a black suit sat straight and tall. He had no head, simply a black button up shirt which covered where his neck stopped. In his hands was a lit jack o'lantern which he set on the desk with the vacant eyes staring at Dory. The mouth was a crooked smile with square teeth, not the happy expression she remembered her father carving on pumpkins on Halloween.

"You're the Landlord," she stated. "That makes sense."

"What do you want?" he barked, his voice emanating from the spot where his head should be.

Dory pulled out her lease, which by now had been folded and unfolded a zillion times. It was less than impressive with its creases and wrinkles, yet was still a binding document. "There was a mistake on my contract," she explained while eying the pumpkin head on the table nervously. The candle within it flickered back and forth, casting horrific shadows within the gourd.

"Don't worry about the jack o'lantern," the Landlord told her. "It's just there for show. Now, what's this about your contract?"

Laying the crinkled paper on the desk, she told him boldly, "It's wrong. I agreed to rent for three months. However, right here . . . " She reached out her right hand as far as she could in order to point at the mistake on the document without going closer to the desk, "Here it says I'm renting for three years."

"I see." the Landlord started to say. He tapped his gloved hand on the desk top. "And you want this corrected?"

"Yeah." Dory said swiftly adding, "Yes, sir."

Frank attempted to jump from her arms, causing Dory to rock a bit. The silver key slipped from her pocket. She quickly stooped over to retrieve it, still holding tightly to Frank within the crook of her left arm.

"I would need a favor from you first. Have you heard of my troubles with the Obnoxious Neighbor upstairs?" He trailed off. Somehow, the headless horseman landlord noticed the shimmering object as she attempted to hide it between her fingers. "Where did you get that key?"

Dory looked down at the silver key in her hand. "Found it," she said, quickly stuffing it into her pocket, thinking back on how the Crazy Cat Lady had reacted to it.

"Hmm," was all that the Landlord said.

"Hmm?" Dory repeated. She waited a moment for the headless horseman to explain himself, but no answer came. "I don't want to deal with the Obnoxious Neighbor," she told him plainly. "What if I just leave?"

"You've already paid me three months' rent which I will not refund. Can you afford to lose three months' rent?" He paused tapping his fingers over the grooves of the pumpkin in front of him. "And where would you go? Most humans only come here because they have no place else to go at the time or they have lived here for decades."

"I . . . " Dory had no argument for his statement. She said once again with more determination, "I won't do this."

"If you don't not help me with this problem, I will not help you," the voice boomed from the collar of the horseman.

"What if I just sued you?" Dory challenged. "You're a landlord. You are supposed to uphold and fix contracts."

"And how will you sue on behalf of your friends?" he bellowed. "Will a courtroom believe that I mistreated a ghost, a vampire, and a werewolf? Or will you simply allow them to live on as they do without the things they need? And can you imagine a headless horseman at the stand? Do you really think that I would appear in court? Now, kick out that Obnoxious Neighbor and to prove to me that you have done this, bring me her roller skate."

"Roller skate?" Dory rubbed her hands across her eyes, imagining stealing some old woman's roller skate for a headless Landlord. Suddenly, she wished she had just made a run for it. She could move in with her parents for a while and just take the financial loss. However, what would become of the three guys? What would happen to other humans in the building if Winston was left unchained or Raleigh set the building on fire as he died? At last, she sighed. "Fine. I'll help you."

"Good. Now go," the voice commanded. The bookshelf door appeared at his command.

Dory started to ask, "But how do I—"

"I said leave!" The words echoed throughout the room and the Landlord tossed his blazing pumpkin head at Dory as she ran for the bookcase. She heard the pumpkin shatter against the inside of the door as she slammed it behind her. Breathing heavily and feeling discouraged, she went down a set of stairs to meet with the others. The secret door led to a little sitting room. A few mismatched chairs were scattered around another passage with a green exit sign hung overhead. Raleigh and Ghost had found Winston propped up on their side of the secret door. They had spent the last ten minutes attempting to revive the werewolf and succeed as Dory entered. When she faced them, the exhaustion of the last few days overwhelmed her. Her eyes welled up with tears and she collapsed into a chair.

"This is so stupid," she complained. "Why can't he just fix things himself? He wants me to go kick out the Obnoxious Neighbor on the thirteenth floor. But the Crazy Cat Lady told me never to go near her. She made it sound like the Obnoxious Neighbor would hurt me if I did."

Raleigh put an arm around Dory's shoulders to comfort her. He leaned his cheek on the top of her head to complete the friendly hug. "Hey, hey. It's going to be okay. He told us all to do the same thing."

Winston instantly added, his features still tinted as green as the walls, "We're all going to go together." He set his hand on Dory's other shoulder and squeezed it.

Ghost looked desperate to also comfort her and hug

her, but his form was too unstable. He leaned down so that his eyes were at her level and said softly, "There's no reason to cry, Dory."

"I'm sorry," she said with a deep inhale. "I can't help it. I just wanted to have this all over and done with."

"And it will be," Ghost told her, "just as soon as we evacuate that Obnoxious Neighbor."

"He told me we have to bring back her roller skate," Dory clarified as she wiped at the last of her tears. "What's that about?"

Raleigh told her, "I've heard the Obnoxious Neighbor used to be a roller derby champion. She sometimes rolls back and forth across the thirteenth floor."

"I've heard it," Winston added. "It's so loud, it sounds like thunder."

Dory shivered. "At least that's semi-normal. Did any of your expect him to be a headless horseman?"

Ghost looked confused, "But the Landlord was a woman, a spirit of a woman with bat wings who was very forward. She kept trying to . . ." Ghost glanced at Dory and a red glow in his translucent cheeks. "Let's just say seduce for a lack of a better word."

"Wait, the Landlord was a succubus?" Raleigh gaped. "How come you got the good one?"

"Why? What was the Landlord when you saw him, or her?" Dory asked. At the same time, she eyed Ghost with a questioning expression that read almost like jealousy.

"He was a giant minotaur," Raleigh told them with disappointment. "But apparently he's a shapeshifter. Winston, what was he to you?"

Rocking a little on his heels at the memory, Winston quickly told them in broken sentences, "Skeleton. Fire. Burning. Not pretty."

"Okay, let's never bring that up again," Dory suggested when she noted Winston's reaction. She then offered everyone a brave look. "Are we ready to go?"

"Ready when you are?" Raleigh told her.

The Marley knocker overheard them and the door beneath the exit sign opened up. It led to a hallway. "The stairs to the eleventh floor are right out there. Remember to come back with the Obnoxious Neighbor's skate, so the Landlord knows that you saw her."

The four started out through door, Dory and Frank in the lead, followed by Ghost, Raleigh, and lastly Winston, who lingered in the doorway. He stood there, calculating days in his head. That night was a full moon.

Chapter Thirteen:
    The Eleventh and Twelfth Floors; The Search for the Obnoxious Neighbor

The eleventh floor was not unlike the other floors in the building. The hallway was long with a staircase leading up to the next floor at the opposite end. Doors lined each side, hiding within them perhaps lives and families or perhaps whatever new horrors waited to mar their journey.

Before anyone could speak or move, a door flew open. A creature which hobbled sideways with great speed and skill came towards them. He had a thin layer of bleach blonde hair atop his greenish scalp. His hands were permanently cupped like little shovels swinging alongside him. He carried with him the sickening rot of a refrigerator full of expired food. He licked his lips at the group, and then glared at Dory and Winston.

"What is that?" Dory screamed as she backed away, picking up Frank on instinct.

Raleigh looked anxious to answer, but seemed at a loss for words as he and Ghost jumped around behind the creature advancing upon the girl and werewolf. Another door in the hallway opened behind them. At first, Winston tensed as the thing approached them, shutting his eyes as if the await a blow to the head. Dory braced her back against the new threat, wondering how she could defend herself while holding her dog. The creature pushed them into the open apartment with a strength strange for his frail form. The door slammed shut, separating them from the hallway.

Setting down Frank, Dory managed to jimmy the handle until it gave way, but by that time, the hallway was empty. She turned back to Winston, but the werewolf had fainted onto the floor.

Not bothering to wake Winston, who had begun to snore, Dory left Frank with him and ran across the hall. She shoved on the door that the creature had come from with her shoulder. The wood crashed into her side, a bruise already beginning to grow. A chain broke on the inside and she tumbled into the apartment, landing on grass. She felt the blades beneath her fingers and sat up with confusion. She was still indoors. The blackish walls met what she assumed was ceiling although clouds rolled across it. A mist crept over the ground, encasing her feet. Sprawled in front of her were rows of tombstones surrounding an old mausoleum. The graves were various shapes and sizes, the names having worn off long ago.

"A graveyard? What's a graveyard doing in here?" Dory moved her way through the granite and marble markers towards the dome shaped mausoleum. "This is ridiculous," she complained. "I can't wait to move out of this house of horrors."

She stepped confidently to the mausoleum's iron doors and flung them open. The hinges squealed in protest. It reminded her of the pictures she had seen of the crypts in New Orleans with the faux Roman columns in front and the black metal decorating the entrance. Inside was a coffin and sitting beside it, tied up in a corner to a giant urn was Raleigh. His eyes glowed in the dark and Dory teased, "You're like a cartoon character."

"Ha ha! Very funny! Now get me out of here," Raleigh hissed with panicked.

"Where's Ghost?" she started to ask, but noticed Raleigh's mouth permanently frozen in a horrified scowl. She knelt down over him, giving his cold cheek a comforting pat. "Why are you so scared? And what was that thing that it could tie you up like this?' Dory questioned as she struggled with the ropes binding him.

"A ghoul," Raleigh explained hurriedly. "They eat dead flesh. He must have smelled us from the hallway. Ghost was solid, so the ghoul thought he was food too, but then Ghost just vanished. It's not like Ghost can be eaten anyway. He's not really here— Maybe that's why he was able to vanish right then."

"Nah, he can just do that sometimes. You know, I've never heard of anything that eats a vampire before," she noted, but Raleigh gave her a warning look. "I mean, that's disgusting," she corrected herself, her fingers slipping through the ropes, straining against the knots.

"Yeah, he's probably going to cut me up so I can't escape and devour me before I can reassemble," Raleigh said with an anxious shudder. "So . . ."

"So?" she repeated as her fingers strained at the knots.

"So, would you please untie me already?"

"Can't you use some of your vampire powers to help me out here?" she grumbled as the ropes refused to slacken.

"When are you going to realize that most of those powers you think I have are based on myths?" Raleigh grumbled.

Dory managed to loosen the ropes while asking, "Isn't anything from the movies true?"

"I did used to wear a cape with a frighteningly high collar." Raleigh pulled his wrists from the ropes and jumped to his feet. "We need to run, now!" The souls of his Italian leather shoes slammed against the marble floor with deafening thuds.

As they moved to the door, the ghoul appeared in the entrance blocking their escape. Raleigh stood behind Dory, but kept his face stoic and brave. "Remember me as I was, a devastatingly handsome bloodsucker with a great sense of style and budding understanding of human emotion."

"Can you shorten that memory a little for us?" a male voice requested from nowhere.

The ghoul looked around, sniffing at the air, but found no one. A hunk of granite broken off one of the crumbling headstones floated over the ghoul's head. At first, the monster bat at it. The stone flew out of reach, and then sped forward, knocking directly into the ghoul's head. It toppled over unconscious, one of its yellow teeth skipping across the floor of the mausoleum towards Dory's red sneaker.

Ghost materialized in front of them, the hunk of stone still in his hands. "Hey guys," he greeted with a smile.

Raleigh tried to pat Ghost gratefully on the back but his hand slipped right through. "Oh, oops." Instead he grinned at him. "Thanks, my good man."

"No problem," Ghost answered.

The three of them exited the ghoul's apartment and retrieved Winston and Frank from across the hall. After reviving the werewolf, they told him the story as the moans of the ghoul waking drifted from the other apartment. Raleigh instantly ran to the end of the hallway. The others followed.

They stumbled in a panic for the steps, only to have a swarm of bats descended over them. Wings and claws caught as a chorus of screeching bit through the calm stairway.

"Why do I feel like someone is trying to stop us from moving towards the thirteenth floor?" Ghost grumbled as a bat few through his head.

The bats screamed and screeched as they flapped their wings at the travelers. Winston pulled his shirt over his head and cried out, "They're in my hair!"

Frank yapped furiously at the bats, hopping back and forth to avoid their tearing feet diving for him. A translucent Ghost uselessly shielded Dory as she yelled out, "They're trying to bite! Who ever heard of bats actually trying to bite people?"

"Let me handle this," the vampire haughtily declared. Raleigh stared down the bats and opened his mouth. The bats wings stuttered as he made a high pitched noise similar to theirs. The round brown bodies retreated out of the hallway as if afraid of him, the flapping of their wings leaving a lingering echo.

They made it up to the twelfth floor and Ghost laughed at the vampire with triumph. "You speak sonar."

"Yep," he simply answered with a pleased smile. "That whole turning into bats myth is based on something true. Vaguely."

Dory narrowed her eyes at him. "What other powers are you holding out on us?"

"I can install a stereo or DVD player in under eight minutes," he told them with the same amount of pride.

Dory nodded. "Okay, if we live through this, you're coming over and hooking up my TV."

Winston meekly added, "Mine too."

They heard the sound of rolling. Everyone turned to look as an army of pumpkins came rolling towards them. They each had different faces carved into their grooved sides and left a trail of seeds in the hallway. They were talking to one another, their voices bouncing off the walls of their hollow shells.

"Chew their toes off!" one of them shouted.

"She ordered us to stop them!" another shouted.

"Leave no toe intact!" a third declared.

"We must leave them without balance!" a forth added.

Raleigh rolled his eyes and Dory shook her head,

muttering, "Seriously?"

Ghost gave Winston a disbelieving look. The werewolf held up a hand, turning it into a paw. "I can handle this one," he told the others.

As the orange gourds spun closer, Winston held up his claw. It caught the florescent light, each tip glistening like a knife. The pumpkins' eye sockets caught hold of the sight and halted. Winston scratched into the wall, pulling out a chunk of wood as if it were soft cake and dropped the piece of wall in front of the pumpkins. Then he wiggled his claw at them. "What was that about chewing off our toes?" The carved faces redirected themselves and vanished down the hallway. The werewolf transformed back into his human shelf and grinned. "That was pretty good right?"

Dory rubbed his back sympathetically. "That was great. Almost makes up for fainting when the ghoul showed up."

Winston nodded in agreement, then realized what the girl had actually said. "I— Hey!"

As they stepped further into the hallway, the lights dimmed. The walls and floor started to shift. Pieces of plaster jutted out, the doors swung open. The hallway changed from a fluorescent lit straight piece of building to a dark, winding passage full of corners and pot holes.

"Ghost, can you turn the lights back on?" Dory called out nervously.

He shook his head then realized that she could not see his movements. "I control electricity. Whatever is happening has nothing to do with wiring."

Raleigh held onto the wall as the hallway at last settled again, "Is everyone okay?"

"What just happened?" Winston asked, regaining his balance.

"Renovations," Ghost stated. "Do you think the Landlord knows about this floor?"

"I think the Landlord knew exactly what was up here," Raleigh accused. "Why do you think he sent us instead of coming himself?"

Hearing the sound of wings beating, Dory pointed upward. "What are those?" she asked with discomfort.

The four things hovered in the corners of the ceiling. Their skin and wings resembled worn brown leather. The creatures were about the size of grown cats, but were built more like deformed children. They had gargoyle like faces and spindly arms. They kept their legs tucked up underneath themselves like stowed landing gear. Their mouths were small, moving back and forth between an o shape to a perfect line as if they were silently mimicking primate chatter.

"Imps," Raleigh groaned in disgust as if they were nothing more than mosquitoes.

"Oh, imps," Ghost repeated as if it were obvious.

"Okay, everyone scatter. There are only four of them." Raleigh pointed to the many nooks and crannies of the corridor. "Hide or keep moving. Just don't let them get to you."

"What do you mean by get to us?" Winston wanted to know. However he discovered the others had already begun running down the hallway. "Hey! Wait for me!" he whined and followed behind.

Raleigh led Dory ahead of him. She carried Frank in her arms. The puppy was eager to play with these strange, ugly birds. "What do imps do if they catch us?" Dory wanted to know, trying to see through the darkness as to where Ghost and Winston had gone.

"Depends on what kind of mischief the imps are into," Raleigh explained.

Dory faced him in time to see one of the creatures hovering behind the vampire's head. "Look out!" she shouted at him.

The imp began to hiss in Raleigh's ear before he could react. "You are a powerful being. You should be ruling over humans. They are food. You are the next step in evolution. You should not have to curb your appetite. Humans should feel honored to be at your mercy." Raleigh seemed hypnotized by the words. He tilted his head in order to listen more carefully. The imp continued, "Animal blood — feh! Animal blood is for mouth breathers with no taste buds. Can't you smell it? That thick, sweet blood coursing in veins so close to you. Yours for the taking. Can't you taste it already? That salty juice dripping from your teeth onto your tongue. That power moving through you, the energy and the life you feel when you stop the heartbeat of a human being. How can you not miss it?"

Raleigh licked his lips. He narrowed his eyes at Dory who instantly backed away. "Raleigh?" She spoke with caution, hoping that he was only pretending. "Raleigh, you like animal blood, remember? Lions, tigers, and bears, remember?"

"Lions are tough eating," Raleigh told her with a smooth voice. He stepped closer to her and smiled a smile that dazzled. "Dory, did I ever tell you how captivating your eyes are?" He attempted to lean his face down to hers. His breath was soft against her cheek and his lips grazed the corner of her lips. "You are really my kind of girl."

Dory flinched. She couldn't help feeling insulted by how easily Raleigh was swayed. She trusted him to control himself. She darkly answered, "What about Georgiana? What would she say if you killed me?"

"Georgiana . . ." Raleigh's eyes softened for an instant.

The imp immediately hissed at Raleigh, "Georgiana, who abandoned you! Who refused your immortal touch! Who married that other man and chose to grow old and die with him! What do you owe that . . . human?"

"Yes—" Raleigh's voice grew distant again. "What do I

owe that human?"

He leaned in once more. His intention on whether to bite or kiss Dory was never determined. She ducked under him, hit him hard in the stomach with her elbow, and ran down the dark hallway. She whip-lashed around a corner where Winston had taken haven. She breathed heavily, not so much out of a need for air but in shock.

"Did you see that? Did you see what he just tried to do?" Dory turned towards Winston, trying to make out his features in the dim light.

His face was fur covered. He opened his mouth wide, his fangs flashing in the little bit of light available. Then Dory noticed a flutter of wings leave his shoulder.

"Oh no, not you too," Dory groaned just as Winston tore his claw through the air in front of her. She whimpered and raced away. Her heart thumped hard against her chest. She felt a pair of hands grasp her arm and pull her behind a wall. She struggled and kicked, but a voice hushed her.

"Dory. Calm down. It's me," Ghost told her. "What's going on?"

"Winston and Raleigh have officially flipped," she explained frantically. "Those little winged things— What did Raleigh call them?"

"Imps. I recognize the word from someplace," Ghost tried to remember. "I do recall something—"

"That they're a pain in the butt?" Dory answered with a whine in her voice.

Ghost glanced out to where their friends were both hunting through the darkness. "Pretty much. They're little demons who—"

"Who manipulate people," she finished. She felt in the dark for Ghost's hand. "They can't get to you, can they?"

"I don't see how. I'm not real. I'm just a memory of a living person. How do you manipulate a memory?" Ghost reasoned with a lopsided grin.

"Governments do it all the time," she replied, squeezing his hand, "it's called history." Her gaze followed his out at the hallway. "So, what are we going to do? I already tried reasoning with Raleigh and it didn't work."

"We run," Ghost told her simply. "It's the most logical plan I can come up with. We run upstairs, deal with that Obnoxious Neighbor and then come back for them on our way back down to the Landlord's apartment." He heard Winston howl and shuddered. "Hopefully they'll be themselves again by then."

"Okay," Dory breathed out in reserved agreement. "On the count of three let's make a run for it. One. Two."

Just then, another imp fluttered over their heads. Dory swatted at it as tiny feet grazed her hair. "Go away!" she futilely cried at the flying demon.

The imp flew over to Ghost's shoulder and began whispering in his ear as the first two imps had done to the others. "You died so unfairly," it told him with deep understanding. "Do you remember? The cold. The falling. You were betrayed. You drowned. You drowned and you should have lived. You had a family that loved you. You had friends that would do anything in the world for you. But that life was taken from you. I don't know how you can stand existing with that kind of pain."

"Ghost, you aren't buying into this, are you?" Dory asked, begging in her voice.

The imp went on, "I know what the siren almost told you; what only some earthbound spirits know." Ghost's eyebrows moved upward with interest. "I know why you would have reason to hurt people." The imp paused again, this time for dramatic effect. Then, it stated slowly and clearly, "Ghosts like you, the ones who died before their time, can form a new body from the slow death of another; from a person whose spirit has already moved onto the afterlife, but their body lingers with a small amount of mortal life."

Unconsciously, Dory took a step away as she glared up at the mangled creature.

Then, as if to punctuate the point with a wicked angle, the imp further added, "If you were to kill the girl, the second her soul left her body, you could form a new body from her shell. You could finally have back the life that was stolen from you."

Dory also heard this. "Whatever happened to two wrongs don't make a right? How does taking my life away before its time make up for the life Ghost lost?"

The imp just laughed at her, "Your life? What makes you think your life is of any importance? He was going to do great things with his life. You just move around a lot and whine about your ideal home."

"I remember," Ghost mumbled in astonishment.

Dory reached for him. She could wrap her hand around his. "Good. That's good, right?" She could not explain why, but she was suddenly terrified of him, yet she held onto his hand tightly.

He pulled away from her and balled both hands into fists. "I was killed. Someone caused me to drive into a river— I drove into the river and no one helped me. I was left alone in that hallway for all of those years!" With eyes like coals, burning from anger and in search of revenge, he looked at her. "It wasn't fair. I deserve a second chance."

"Yes, you do. And I'll help you with that. But first, we have to do this," Dory attempted to reason with him. The spirit moved towards her, his hands now stretched out in front of him, aimed for her slender neck. "Ghost! Ghost, is it really logical for you to kill me and take my body! You'll be alive, but you won't have any friends. You'll still be alone."

She could see conflict in his face. In a moment of hesitation, Ghost dropped his hands. His eyes still glared at her like she had been his murderer all of those years ago. She used the opportunity to run, dashing away from him in a blind panic. Dory dodged doors and jumped over holes beneath her. Frank squeaked at each jarring motion and she squeezed him more tightly against herself. She could see the stairs to the thirteenth floor were not far off. The imps chased her down. They surrounded and cornered her against the wall nearest the staircase.

An imp slightly larger than the others swooped down in front of her. "Stay away from me," she meaninglessly warned.

The larger imp stared into her eyes. She avoided his gaze, but the creature moved a little away from her. The imp bowed its head at Dory. "We can't influence you," it admitted, its voice was small and raspy as if Dory had strangled it.

With obvious distrust, she asked, "Why? What makes me different from the others?"

"That kiss on your forehead," the imp told her, not daring to look up at her.

"Kiss?" Dory rubbed at her forehead as if the kiss were a bump she could feel. She remembered the Crazy Cat Lady giving her the kiss before she left her apartment and thinking about how awkward it was. "What does that kiss have to do with anything?"

"The kiss was a wish to protect you. It was an act of caring," the imp clarified. "It might be corny, but we can't work against something like that."

"Oh." Dory looked around them, trying to find an escape. "Does that mean you're going to let me go?"

"No. It just means that we are going to bring you to her as you are," the imp made clear. He reached out both of his arms like a toddler wanting a hug. "If you would come along quietly, it would be greatly appreciated."

The other imps all nodded their heads in unison, each

one made as nervous by the kiss on Dory's forehead as the one who spoke to her. She begrudgingly agreed to come with them. The flying demons gathered around her, reminding her of a twisted parody of the winged cherubs in Victorian paintings. "What happens to my friends?" she wanted to know as they imps lead her through the darkness to the stairs.

"She wants to have the werewolf as a guard dog," the imp responded. "The others will be left here."

"Will they be okay? I mean, are Raleigh and Ghost going to go up and down the halls trying to kill people for blood and bodies?" she wanted to know, thinking how horrified both men would be with themselves after they awoke from their trances.

"They'll be fine," the imp declared with a certain amount of mischief and pride. "Our sway over them will fade as soon as we are back on the thirteenth floor."

Dory paused on the stairs on the way up to the next floor. Petting Frank on the head, she uneasily asked the imp, "So, she really does know some magic. That's how she controls you guys, right?"

At first, the creature twisted his nose at her for her impertinent question. Still, he answered, unable to stop his chatter, "She has something of ours. We're in her service until she no longer has the object," the imp explained. "But yes, she does have a certain amount of power. Most of it comes from her being a bitch, though. There seems to be amazing powers that come with that."

Despite her anger at the evil little spirits, Dory found herself smiling at the imp's observation. She finished the trek to the thirteenth floor and allowed the imp to take her into the Obnoxious Neighbor's apartment.

Chapter Fourteen:
  The Thirteenth Floor; The Rescue

Heavy metal music blared throughout the expansive apartment. The bass thudded, forcing the shelves on the walls to jiggle and dance. Dory stood in what she assumed was a sitting room hidden amongst decades upon decades of trash, boxes, and nick-nacks. Posters advertising extreme sporting events were pasted as closely together as possible like wallpaper. The floor had not been vacuumed or swept in some time. Dory could make out the lines left in the dirt from a pair of roller skates constantly crossing the floor. A section of one wall was covered with a collage of Polaroid photographs each one revealing some small aspect of each of the apartment tenants' lives. It was obvious the shots were taken from awkward angles, some through vents, others through keyholes, and even a couple from the other side of windows.

"She spies on everyone," Dory murmured to herself, recognizing her own face, slightly blurred by a far off shot from days earlier when she had been moving into her new apartment.

Ghost did not appear in any of the photos, but there were glimpses of Winston's paw reaching around from within his apartment door for his newspaper and of Raleigh exiting his apartment with a large, confident stride. Most pictures were of the green door outside of the Landlord's apartment. The Obnoxious Neighbor must have spent a great deal of time attempting to capture the whatever he, she, or it was on film. The closest she had come was a blur of a leg ducking back into the apartment door. The Obnoxious Neighbor had thumb tacked copies of the Landlord's newsletters like the one Dory had seen in the Crazy Cat Lady's apartment in chronological order. Messy red circles and neon highlighter marks painted each newsletter in chaos, like the Obnoxious Neighbor was road mapping a conspiracy through the fluff articles and pieces of obvious, easily manipulated advice. Dory began to realize why the neighbor made the Landlord so nervous. The former roller derby champion was after something and she had obsessively targeted him.

A woman entered, slipping around the trash in the room like an expert cat burglar. She had wild graying hair which was pulled up in a high pony tail, then splayed around her head like a frame. She dressed as a punk rocker, complete with nose ring and tattoos. The sleeves of her shirt had been removed then safety pinned back to the bodice. She was missing an eye which she covered with a silver-studded patch. The eye could have been the result of a roller derby mishap in her younger years. Her finger nails were painted electric blue and she had painted foundation an inch thick across her face. She glared at Dory through long fake eyelashes, bits of glue still visible at the edges. The music blared through the apartment, yet it seemed insignificant compared with the woman's appearance.

The Obnoxious Neighbor rounded on Dory. "So, you're the one in my sister's apartment." Her voice carried easily over the music. She critically sized up the young woman and then shook her head with disapproval. "Pathetic," she grumbled, then returned to her easy chair.

Dory wrinkled her nose at the neighbor, insulted. "Excuse me?" She strained to talk over the pounding bass and banging drums. "What do you think is so pathetic?"

"You, of course." She sighed as if she felt some sort of

pity towards Dory's apparent pathetic-ness. She then stepped closer, smelling like cigarettes and scotch. "You think you're pretty clever, don't you."

"Yes, but what does that have to do with anything?" Dory replied with a shaky voice.

The Obnoxious Neighbor held out her hand palm up to Dory. "Give it to me," she stated plainly. "I know you must have found it. I know that ridiculous Landlord doesn't have it which means you must have found it."

"Found what?" Dory asked, attempting to move away from the woman's grabby hands.

"The key!" the Obnoxious woman coldly replied. Her fingers twitched in anticipation. "The silver key."

Dory refrained from touching her pocket of the dress where she still had the key hidden away. "I don't have any key except the key to my apartment and I need that." She moved a little ways away, placing a table between herself and the Obnoxious Neighbor.

With insistence, the Obnoxious Neighbor explained, "Did you really think you could just come into my home and shove me out? I've lived here almost as long as anyone else! You can't just make me leave! I should be in charge of this building of freaks, not that hermit!" She paused to await the girl's opinion, but Dory did not respond. The woman reached her hands further into Dory's personal space. Snatching up the young woman's arm, the neighbor twisted until Dory felt her muscles stain and bruise, her bones reaching their breaking point. "I'm warning you. Give me that key or I'll—"

Dory pushed away from her and jutted out her chin. "You'll what? You can't do anything to me," the young woman boldly challenged. "You're not like Raleigh or Ghost or Winston and you aren't some witch in a fairy tale. You're a human being and if you hurt me you'll have to answer to the law."

The Obnoxious Neighbor took a step backwards and chuckled. She rounded the table, heading towards the door. "The law? And does the law know that you're currently here, my dear?"

Dory's eyes fell, but her chin stayed upwards in defiance. "People would notice if I disappeared," she said slowly, hoping that the words would have more power than they truly did. She wondered if anyone was already looking for her. She'd been walking through the building for days without a phone or any contact to the outside world.

Her captor released a low grumble, her single eye rolling upwards towards the ceiling with annoyance. The Obnoxious Neighbor tapped a long nailed finger across the table top. "Very well. You have an hour to decide on what you want to do. You can either give me that key or face the consequences. Your choice, my dear." She then leaned down and gathered Frank roughly into her arms. "Hmm, collateral," she murmured as the dog whimpered.

The older woman exited before the young woman could put up a fight. Dory was left with the sounds of the whirling machinery from old VCRs stacked in corners and broken clocks with stuck second hands straining to tick. The bass of the music still pounded against the boundaries of the apartment. Dory sunk down on the floor, the skirt and petticoat gathering up around her like a blanket. She took the key from her pocket. Laying the silver object in her flat palm, Dory inspected it carefully. So much trouble over something so small. Was it worth protecting? She didn't even know what it was for. Yet, the Crazy Cat Lady's warnings nagged at her mind and her gut reminded her that she should not give up the key to anyone.

Realizing that the old woman might be watching her, Dory re-pocketed the key and ran for the door. It was locked tight and would not budge. There were no windows and the only other door was the one leading to wherever the Obnoxious Neighbor had gone. She settled down on the floor again, letting the thick petticoats protect her from the grime. She wanted to cry, yet her pride kept a drought in her eyes.

Pulling her knees up close to her chest, Dory murmured to herself, "What do I do?"

She wished her mom was there to give her advice and that her dad was nearby with the supportive pat on the back. Dory's mind wandered to her new friends and her wish altered. Rubbing her arm which pulsated with the burn of nearly being snapped by the Obnoxious Neighbor, Dory realized that even in elementary school, when she the other kids picked on her for her clothes or hair, she ran to her parents, not her playmates. In college, when something went wrong with an unfair professor or an overbearing boss, she held onto it until she was home for a weekend. Even her ex-boyfriend, the loon, never bothered to help her when she needed it and she never asked him for any.

Dory had to face facts. In two days, the three monsters had treated her with more caring than her oldest chums. A part of her wanted the thought to uplift her, to make her stand up for herself and never say die. Instead, her depression weighed upon her as the life she was trying to get back to suddenly seemed less appealing.

"Please let them find me," she whispered.

The hour passed quickly and the woman returned. She had a piece of rope tied around Frank's neck. She dragged the little dog into the room while whistling a Black Sabbath song. As Frank yelped, Dory jumped back up.

"Don't hurt my dog!"

"Give me the key!" the woman snapped back.

"I can't," Dory answered with renewed courage.

"Well then, I'm sorry, but the dog dies," she said without any remorse.

Dory's hands balled into fists and she pursed her lips.

Her heartbeat raced, thudding within her like the bass of the woman's loud music. "You're not obnoxious, you're just mean!" she shouted. The words seemed childish, but Dory continued anyway, thinking back on all of the people she had run to her parents for help with; the school persecutors, the tyrannical professors, and even her crazy ex-boyfriend before they hauled him away. She never really stood up to any of them herself. Yet, she had criticized a ghost, scolded a vampire, and slapped a werewolf.

"And you know what, you're not that annoying! I've had neighbors ten times worse than you!" The young woman lifted her right fist into the air squarely punch the Obnoxious Neighbor in the nose.

The old woman stumbled backwards onto the floor, completely stunned. She began to wail like an angry bully bested on the playground. "You hit me!" she screamed. "No one hits me!"

As she yowled, her body began to shrink. First, she reduced down to the size of an eight year old child. Then further, her arms and legs staying proportionate as her body decreased in size. Her face remained in that old woman scowl and the volume of her voice got quieter and quieter, going up octaves in pitch the smaller she was. Soon, she was the size of Frank who was jumping back and forth, watching excitedly. In another moment, she was the size of a penny, then a dime, and then she was gone. Dory's eyes widened, trying to comprehend what she had just seen. She opened her mouth, wondering if she spoke to herself the situation would make more sense. Instead all she managed to utter was, "Oh."

The door burst open a few minutes later, the deadbolt breaking through the door frame and leaving wood splinters on the floor. Ghost had a piece of door in his hands, ready to beat any surprises down. Raleigh's fangs were protruding from his gums and he snarled for effect.

Winston was a full werewolf, leaping in behind them and growling angrily.

"Where is that Obnoxious Neighbor?" Raleigh demanded.

Winston roared, the werewolf equivalent of "Let me at her!"

Ghost moved directly next to Dory asked, "Are you alright?"

She was still staring at the spot where the woman had been, her mouth hanging open and her eyes wide. "S . . . she shrunk," Dory at last told them, not certain if she believed her own words. Her stinging knuckles were the only proof of what she had done.

Somehow, Dory's shock calmed down the three men. Ghost breathed a sigh, Raleigh's shoulders relaxed, and Winston partially transformed back into a human. His height reduced down slightly and he stood upright, but thanks to the full moon, fur and claws remained behind.

"What did you say?" the werewolf asked, also staring at the empty spot on the floor where Dory's attention remained fixed.

"She shrunk into nothing. She was right there and then she got smaller and smaller and smaller until poof! She was gone," Dory explained to them.

Each of them raised their eyebrows and shook their heads. Raleigh spoke first, "Dory, people don't just shrink."

"Well, she did! Honestly, after everything we've seen you're questioning shrinking people?" she told them back, her shock being overcome by irritation.

"Never heard of it happening," Raleigh explained, "and I've heard it all."

"It does seem pretty farfetched," Winston added, leaning down and sniffing the spot they had been staring at.

She looked at Ghost. "You believe me don't you?"

He rubbed the back of his neck nervously. "Honestly? It really doesn't seem logical that she would just . . . shrink like that."

Dory let out a noise, a half squeak, half gasp, her express her anger at them. "Why would I make this up?"

"You've been through a lot," Ghost reasoned. "Maybe you just think you saw her shrinking."

"Of course I think that," Dory argued pointing at the floor. "You know why? Because she shrunk!"

Winston avoided her eyes. "Um, we should get back to the Landlord."

"Yeah, where's that roller skate?" Raleigh said, busying himself by looking through each box and under every piece of furniture.

Dory huffed. "Some friends," she grumbled.

Just then a jack o'lantern rolled into the room. "You shrunk her!" he proclaimed.

Tossing up her hands in triumph and letting out a victorious, "Ha!" Dory added to her three friends, "See, I told you!" A second later, she sobered and looked nervously down at the jack o'lantern. "Wait. Am I in trouble for this? Are you guys going to try and gnaw off my toes now?"

"Are you kidding?" the jack o'lantern laughed happily. "We couldn't be more thrilled! Toes taste disgusting, but we had to do what she said or she'd smash us. Thank you!"

"Oh," Dory said relaxing. "You're welcome then." She turned her stare back to the three men who were each stooped over going through piles of garbage around the room. "And what do you have to say for yourselves?"

"Have you found that roller skate yet?" Raleigh asked pulling out an old sock with a red sucker hanging from the heel.

The other two in unison answered, "Not yet." None of the men would meet her gaze, ignoring the sound of her grinding teeth.

Dory crossed her arms over her chest and darkly told them, "You three are in so much trouble."

Chapter Fifteen:
The Thirteenth Floor; The Winged Imps

They rummaged for food while they sought the Obnoxious Neighbor's roller skates. The kitchen was just as messy as the rest of the apartment, so all food was consumed with caution. They found a couple of uncooked steaks in her refrigerator which Winston mutilated raw while Raleigh lapped up the blood from the packaging. Dory found some bread and peanut butter. She made herself a sandwich and threw the crusts to Frank.

Raleigh stood up to search more as he skillfully licked his fingers. "Let's find that skate and get out of here."

Winston also stood looking around apartment with horror. His long, fluffy wolf's tail was tucked between his legs revealing any timidity his voice tried to hide. "This place is disgusting. I don't really want to keep digging." He was easily distracted by a pile of dirty dishes. As he walked passed the sink's pile, staring at it intently, his foot collided with something unstable. He tripped, rolled, and landed flat on his back.

"Good job," Raleigh praised. "You found them. Now we can go."

Dory thought over her situation, remembering the words of the imps. She was there with three guys she barely knew, all of whom could harm her in some way. Raleigh was asking for a high five from Ghost, the one hand passing directly through the other. Winston laughed, then held up his own hand in dorky eagerness. Raleigh and

Ghost both looked at him a little skeptically, but did not leave the werewolf hanging. Dory giggled as Winston fell forward in his attempt to slap his paw against Ghost's non-existent palm.

College was the last time Dory remembered having fun with people who weren't her family or her dog. She wondered if any of them were having a good time in their high profile jobs or in their new locations.

Raleigh came to stand beside her as Ghost put on a comical performance in trying to pick Winston back up. As his hands kept slipping directly through Winston, Ghost would jest, "Well, how did that happen? What are you doing on the floor? Just grab my hand, Winston."

She glanced at the vampire near her. "Think everything is going to be alright now? The Landlord is going to fix everything, right?"

"Course," Raleigh replied. "I just hope I get the succubus this time."

"You can have her," Ghost answered eying Dory with embarrassment. "She was pushy and trashy." Dory raised an eyebrow at him accusingly. He then hung his head and admitted, "I guess she was kinda pretty."

"Seriously?" Winston piped up as he got off the floor. "Pushy and trashy? Maybe she'd like a guy who's tidy and submissive? Opposites attract."

"I already called dibs," Raleigh told the other two with a determined shake of his head.

Rolling her eyes, Dory decided it was time to burst their bubble. "May I remind you all that this was the same being that was the monster, the skeleton, and the headless horseman, all of who I assume were males. Are you guys really going to hit on something that was a man three out of four times?"

Winston and Ghost both shook their heads no, but Raleigh thought over the matter seriously. "Nope, doesn't bother me," he concluded.

The others all nodded their heads casually. "Okay, that's cool," they each said.

As Dory held the roller skate by the laces, it hit her leg when she moved. She could feel the wheels rolling through the petticoats of her dress. "Are we ready to face the dangers of the last two floors again?" The guys all groaned and Dory leaned over, debating on taking only one of the roller skates or the pair. She reached down to where the roller skates had been stashed under a counter. Also hidden in the open cupboard was a metal helmet. Carved into the iron was an old pattern reminding Dory of pictures her history teacher showed her of early Britain before the Middle Ages. She held the helmet into the light. The sound of leathery wings beating filled the apartment. The imps entered and perched on the tops of furniture throughout the home.

"Oh great," Winston shuddered. "They're back!" He plugged his fingers into his ears and hummed loudly, "You can't influence me! I don't have to listen! La la la! HUM!"

"It's a full moon, you're almost fully wolf, and you're touching garbage," Raleigh pointed out. "I'm more worried about you spazzing out than you killing any of us."

Winston glowered at Raleigh, yet secretly adrenaline and pride pumped through his veins. There was a full moon outside and he was mostly transformed, but he didn't feel angry or violent. The need to kill had yet to come to his muscled arms and fierce claws.

Dory held out the Celtic helmet to the imps. "Is this what she was using to control you?"

"It is," the main imp stated, his eyes shining upon the object, "And I am bound to tell you that because you now hold it, you are now in control of us."

"Oh, Dory! Let me see that!" Raleigh shouted excitedly, making a grab for the helmet. "It's payback time, you little winged rats!"

Pulling the helmet out of the vampire's reach, Dory decidedly told him, "No. I think they can help us."

The three young men looked doubtful. They watched the imps carefully, making sure that they never had their back to a single one of them. Each time one would move to a different part of the ceiling, they would shift their positions and back further against a wall.

"Could you help us?" Dory asked the main imp.

"With what?" he asked with curiosity.

"We need to get back down to the tenth floor. The Landlord is expecting us." She noticed how the imp pretended not to hear her. With a sigh, Dory placed the helmet onto her head. She could hear her own breathing bouncing off of the metal and the hat had the thick, earthy smell of iron. Speaking with a great deal of annoyance and exhaustion, she commanded, "Will you please take us safely to the Landlord's apartment on the tenth floor?"

The main imp rubbed the back of his nails against his chest. "We have to do it. You're wearing the helmet. Seems a waste of our abilities though . . . "

Ghost smirked, "Well, if you can't do it—"

"Oh, don't try that mind game on us," the main imp proclaimed as he motioned for three of his companions to lift the Ghost up into the air. "We invented that mind game."

Four imps lifted Winston into the air and another three picked up Raleigh. Both grunted nervously. The main imp supported Dory's shoulders while others lifted her up by her legs, arms and back. Frank curled up on her stomach as if she were a hammock.

The imps flew them out of the door and down the stairs to the previous floor. As they passed over the treacheries of the uneven floor and dark hall, Dory asked, "Do you have any idea why this building so full of—"

"Unusual creatures such as us and your friends there?" the imp finished for her. "I know a story. Should I tell it to you?"

"Yes, please," she answered and listened carefully as the imps slowly flew them through the twelfth floor.

"This neighborhood was once the city's ethnic stew pot of the old world. Immigrants from all over Europe settled in this area and had children and passed down their traditions," the imp told her, with all the flair of a professional storyteller despite his raspy voice. "They also passed down their old fears and superstitions.

"A man was commissioned to design this building here. The man took the project, especially when he was told that he and his beautiful bride would be allowed to live in the building free of charge when it was finished. However, the more he learned about the neighborhood, the more he feared for his wife."

"Wasn't she a fan of having Italians and Irishmen as neighbors?" Dory asked carefully as they soared passed the sleeping bats on the stairs and down to the eleventh floor.

"Oh no. She was very excited about living here," the imp explained, "But her husband knew how they would react to her. She was a very gifted fortune teller and extremely skilled with herbs and plants. In short, she was a witch. He knew that the neighborhood would fear her as they did all of their old world stories. While he designed the building, he decided to make it his wife's haven. He declared that it would always be a safe place for those like her with powers the world did not fully understand."

"And it stayed that way all this time," Dory commented. "That's a very nice story." She thought about the man's young wife being able to escape to her home any time someone made her feel persecuted or weird. "Do you know, were they happy?"

"Oh, very happy," the imp added losing the style from

his tone. "If you like that boring sort of thing." They hovered for a moment at the top of the stairs leading down to the next floor, waiting for the imps carrying her friends to finish their own decent.

As they floated down the stairs and the main imp set Dory down in front of the Landlord's door on the tenth floor, she asked him, "Don't you like being happy?"

The creature made a noise at the back of his throat as if he was about to cough something up onto her head. "Happy? What good is happy if you don't have the occasional unhappy to compare it to? In my professional opinion, most people who say they are happy all of the time lead very boring lives." Squinting one eye at Dory, he said, "You wouldn't be thinking of living a boring life, would you?"

Smiling at him, she sighed, "I'll keep what you said in mind." Waving the helmet at him and the other imps, she added, "Thanks. I'll call for you if we need you again." The imps flew off.

Raleigh turned to the door and mumbled, "I need a bath."

Winston added without thinking, "Yeah, you smell like imp."

Chapter Sixteen:
The Tenth Floor; The Discovery of the Landlord

The Marley knocker greeted them with the same cold professionalism as before. "You lived," he said with surprise. "Very well. I'll announce you."

The four entered the impressive apartment once more, but did not sit in the chairs. They stood around the table offering each other comforting looks despite the fact that each of them was worried about the same thing. What would happen if the Landlord still refused them?

After a nerve wracking fifteen minutes, the Marley knocker's voice boomed throughout the apartment. "The Landlord will see you now."

"Which one of us?" Winston wanted to know, feeling Dory grasp his arm.

"All of you. Together," the voice told them. "You may enter as a group"

Dory glanced back at Frank to make certain the little dog followed them as they headed down the wide hallway shoulder to shoulder. The roller skate swayed against her, weighing down her right hand. The laces twisted through her fingers and cut off the circulation still her grip did not slacken.

Raleigh knocked. The door was opened carefully and they stepped inside to face the back of the desk chair. The group waited with baited breath as the chair turned. Ghost anticipated the succubus and kept glancing at Dory as if to wait for her reaction. Raleigh was convinced that the

Minotaur would show up. He puffed himself up a little, ready for a fight. Winston was wincing, waiting for the burning skeleton to show his flaming head. Lastly, Dory readied herself for the sight of the headless horseman.

The chair pivoted and sitting within the green leather was nothing. The chair appeared to be empty.

"Is this a joke?" Raleigh wanted to know.

The Landlord's voice came from everywhere, similar to how the Marley knocker spoke to them from within the apartment. "No joke, vampire. Why have you all come back here so soon?"

"Where are you?" Winston wanted to know, his head moving frantically.

"In the chair," the Landlord's voice answered. The chair twitched a little as if to support his words.

"He's invisible," Ghost clarified. "Hey, I can do that trick too."

"I repeat," the Landlord said, ignoring Ghost's comment, "why are you back so soon? Have you given up?"

"No," Dory told him as the others still wrapped their minds around the Landlord's many forms, "We did what you said." She held the roller skate up and tossed it onto the desk. "We got rid of the Obnoxious Neighbor."

There was a pause. Then the Landlord spoke with obvious trepidation. "She is gone."

"And not coming back," Raleigh added. "How about keeping your promises?"

Without skipping a beat, the Landlord answered, "Of course. Return to the guest rooms and I will think over the matter. We shall speak again tomorrow."

"Tomorrow?" Winston repeated with a withered expression.

Dory took a step closer to the desk, "You can't keep us waiting like this!"

"Oh, but I can," the Landlord answered. "You should

feel honored that I have granted you each audience at all!"

As the voice boomed angrily, Frank busied himself at the edge of the bookshelf behind the desk. The little dog stumbled over a lever connecting the wheels of the chair to the bottom of the bookcase. The wall opened up to revealed a large room full of wires, levers, buttons, and pulleys. In the midst of the equipment, a balding man in his early seventies sat on a rickety stool. His hands hung onto different wheels and frantically tried to make the wall turn back. "Pay no attention to that man behind the bookcase!" he ordered.

"Who's that?" Winston asked pointing at the man.

"I think that's the Landlord," Ghost stated with upset.

Raleigh shook his head instantly. "No. No, the Landlord is a powerful being, a feared and—"

"A fraud," Dory muttered hanging her head.

The little old man stumbled out from the center of the machinery. "Yes," he said, shamefully, "I am the Landlord."

Raleigh snarled at the man and pouted, "No succubus. What a jip!"

"Did you mean anything you told us?" Winston wanted to know, a growl forming in his voice.

The Landlord held his hands in front of him defensively, obviously afraid of the three monsters before him. "No. No. I'm just not everything I said I was. I needed to say something to survive." He pointed backwards into the little cupboard in the bookshelves. The levels and pulleys were surrounded by television screens, one for each apartment living room. "I really do try to keep an eye on things though."

Dory faced him down, tears at the edges of her eyes. "All those tricks. All of those lies. They were all just to protect yourself from your own tenants. That's why you wanted the Obnoxious Neighbor gone. She was onto you. That's why her apartment was full of photos of your door.

She was trying to catch you and prove how human you are. She wanted to prove you were lying to everyone!"

The little man rose from the stool, wringing his hands. "Yes, she wanted the landlord position for herself. She would've made an awful landlord. I was just trying to protect everyone." He tried to straighten up and show a little courage. "And I had to protect myself! Have you seen the freaks that live in this building?" The Landlord defended, and then quickly turned to the three men in the room, his posture shrinking again, "No offense."

Winston shrugged, "Eh, I know I'm a freak."

"Yeah, because you're obsessive and suffer from anxiety attacks," Raleigh put in. "Come on. I'm the blood sucking fiend here."

Ghost scoffed. "I don't even have a name or a complete past. What makes you two think you're freaks?"

Dory snapped at them, "None of you are freaks, got it." They all hung their heads. She then turned to the Landlord and repeated, "They aren't freaks and if you'd go out of your apartment every once in a while or actually talked to your neighbors instead of just spying on them, you might know that." She glanced again at the television screens. "In fact, you're the freakiest person we've met in this building. And yes, that's including the ghoul and the Obnoxious Neighbor! At least that roller derby bitch only took photos of people's comings and goings. You're a full blown peeping Tom!"

"Wow," Raleigh breathed, impressed. "She's pissed."

"Maybe we should stand back," Winston observed as Dory threw her arms in the air as a part of her rant.

"Quite frankly, Mr. Landlord," she said, the word mister drawn out like she was sickened by it, "I think you're a pretty awful human being!"

The Landlord's face fell. He muttered the words, "That is very harsh, young woman. Just because I used some props and some smoke and mirrors to help you each see something amazing, that doesn't make me a bad person."

"Oh yeah?" Raleigh scoffed. "Then how did you end up here in the first place that you had to . . . set all this up?"

The Landlord motioned to the room behind the bookcase where a giant animatronics Minotaur was set on a platform beside a projector playing slides of a winged woman and a giant marionette of a skeleton. A headless horseman costume hung a hook on the wall.

With a sigh, as if he needed a moment to remember the truth after so many years of lies, the Landlord explained. "At one time I was a special effects designer for some of the top film studios. But then they started to switch to computers and I was forced into early retirement. I moved into this apartment building by accident," the Landlord explained. "I applied for the job of landlord when the old landlord mistook me for a hobgoblin." The Landlord glanced down at his pot belly and stubby legs. "Which is also quite harsh. It didn't take me long to figure out that I was running a madhouse. I was getting complaints from monsters of all kinds. I was terrified of one of them eating me, so I figured I better make sure I was more intimidating than all of them."

"And nothing is more worrying than a mystery," Ghost clarified. "You became the unknown in a building full of unknowns. Good job."

"Don't encourage him," Dory sickly told Ghost.

"What encouraging?" Ghost defended, "I'm not encouraging, I'm just commenting."

Raleigh added, "Dory, we know you're upset, but let's hear the man out."

Surprised by the vampire's soft, understanding tone, Dory shut her lips tightly and rested her head in her hands while leaning on the Landlord's desk.

The Landlord went on, "I sent out newsletters to the

human residents so they felt I was still helping them, even if they never saw me. I used camera equipment in the hallways to watch out for danger. I saw the way the four of you worked together. I knew you could help me with the problem with the Obnoxious Neighbor. She was going to destroy it all."

"She knew what you were," Dory realized.

"She was blackmailing me," he grumbled with distaste. "Despicable woman."

Ghost shook a scolding finger at the Landlord. "You gave her what she wanted and in exchange she didn't set all the evils of this building against you."

Raleigh added, "But it wasn't enough for her. She wanted to be in charge."

"Probably to punish all the people who were always complaining about her," Winston added.

"Exactly." He sheepishly stared at her from under bushy gray eyebrows. "I am sorry for lying to you though."

The ghost, the werewolf, and the vampire were quiet. Dory said what they were all thinking. "And what about the things you promised us? It's not like you could fix any of our problems without leaving your apartment. Were you just going to keep stalling until you could find a way to get rid of us too?"

The Landlord rubbed his stubbly old chin thoughtfully. "Come with me," he told them and lead the group into the room of gadgets behind the bookcase.

Chapter Seventeen:
The Tenth Floor; The Tricky Art of the Great Fraud

The secret room was a miniature prop house. There were costumes, masks, puppets, gears, and everything needed to make an explosion that would tear down the building. A window let in the moonlight for them to see by.

As he wound them through boxes and crates, the Landlord pointed to a work table made of dusty pine wood. "Well, let's go back over what you each wanted," the Landlord suggested. He turned to Ghost first. "You wanted to be able to roam free throughout the building so you could find a person to frighten. Personally, I think that you could scare anyone with all of that talking you do. You're a very smart young man. If you put your mind to it, you could manage anything."

Ghost seemed pleased by this compliment, yet still anxious for official answer.

The Landlord went on, "All the same, your wish is granted. You have permission to haunt on which ever floor you choose. And to give you proof, I present to you . . ." As the old man spoke, he had begun to fill out a small, rectangular piece of paper about the size of a driver's license. He then walked over to a large machine, a bit like a Xerox machine, but instead giant sheets of plastic were fed into it. He put the rectangle inside, then waited for the machine to spit it back out. He then handed the laminated card to Ghost. "I give you a hall pass, signed by me and good for an eternity."

"Hey, that's pretty neat," Ghost awed, holding the lamination up to the moonlight. "Thanks."

Dory rolled her eyes at the absurd gift. "At least Ghost seems happy about it. I don't know how he's going to carry that around when he's transparent though," she muttered to Frank.

Raleigh stepped forward. "What about my problem?"

The Landlord set his hand on Raleigh's shoulder. "You wish to have the windows in your apartment better covered so you don't have to feel pain from the sunshine." Raleigh nodded earnestly. The Landlord looked the vampire in the eyes. "You seem to already suffer from a great deal of pain. On top of immortality, you have loss and caring and worry for others to burden you. I think for a vampire with such emotion, the sun should be your last worry. I'll have a maintenance man cover your windows in metal sheeting first thing tomorrow." He pulled the metal sheeting out from under the work table. "Be sure to leave this outside of the apartment door." He called upward, "Marley, be sure to tell maintenance."

"Of course, sir," the knocker's voice responded.

Raleigh's head slowly pivoted to look at the Landlord. "You really think I have human emotions?" He was stunned.

The Landlord rubbed his hand along the edge of his hairline, small beads of sweat rubbing against his fingers. "Yes, yes. You poor man. I know that if I for one was faced with an eternity, I would want all that messy emotional business out of my way."

Sheepishly, Raleigh sort of shrugged it off, like his emotions were no big deal. "You, um, you better help Winston next." He pointed to the werewolf who was anxiously pulling on his shirt with a furry claw, tearing a hole in the cotton.

Rubbing his chin, the Landlord murmured, "Yes. You

want to be able to lock yourself up when your transformations are getting out control."

Winston glanced at the others as if he needed their encouragement in order to speak. "Actually, I think I can control it better now. Tonight is a full moon and I've managed to stay somewhat human most of the night. But I'd still like something, just in case."

The Landlord smiled a warm smile at the werewolf. "You are very brave to attempt to face such a transformation."

"I am?" Winston asked with wonder.

"Yes," the Landlord went on. "You have a great deal to be proud of. You are a bold creature to dare leaving your apartment and even bolder to try for so long not to ever leave out of fear of hurting someone. It's scary being on your own all the time. I should know. So, I have a gift for you as well." He walked over to a seven foot tall rectangle under an old canvas sheet. Removing the cover, a cage with thick steel bars towered before them. One side of it made up a hinged door kept closed with a built in combination lock. "This cage was once used to hold two gorillas in a jungle picture I was working on. If it could keep them trapped I'm sure it'll work for you. When you're human you'll be able to work the door and the combination lock in order to get yourself in and out."

"But when I'm the wolf I won't be able to break the bars or pick the lock," Winston finished with elation. "Thanks. Thanks a lot."

The Landlord chuckled at his gratitude. "Yes well, be sure to put it outside of the apartment door and maintenance will deliver it to your home for you." He wrote down the combination and handed the scrap of paper to Winston.

Ghost moved over to where the fourth member of their group had been watching with patience and pride.

"What about Dory?"

Raleigh added, "Yeah. Fix Dory's lease."

Winston put in, "Yeah! Give her a chance to get out of this mad house."

The Landlord opened his mouth wide as he thought. His bottom jaw hung for a moment as he made a long "awww" sound. At last, he stopped thinking and answered. "The fact of the matter is that I can't actually change your lease," he told her. "I don't write them. Gilda does."

Dory eyes fell. Sensing the disheartening trance she was slipping into, Ghost asked in her place, "Who is Gilda?"

The Landlord pointed upward as if the mysterious Gilda could hear them. "Her grandfather designed this building. She always allows a landlord to run things so long as she was made aware of all deals. Therefore, she writes up the contracts and only she could change it for you." He allowed a wistful smile to peek through his guilt. "She's quite a character, though. She reads tarot cards and sews quilts for homeless shelters. She could tell you some amazing stories . . . if you're on her good side. Of course, as far as she knows I'm a talking boar."

Ghost chuckled, the sound laden with more shock than humor. "You even lied to her. Wow. Talk about employee trust."

With a complete lack of enthusiasm, Dory asked, "Where can we find her?"

"Top floor." He set his hand on Dory's shoulder. "You will have to convince her, my dear. I'm sure the problem with your lease was no accident. I don't think she does anything by accident."

Winston and Raleigh took their gifts out to the hallway, which was difficult for Winston whose cage had to be jiggled and tilted through the doorways. Ghost stayed with Dory in the Landlord's prop house. She was playing with Frank on the sawdust covered floor, but not speaking.

"It'll work out," he assured her.

"I'm afraid of turning out like him," she muttered. Her eyes stayed locked upon patterns in the dusty floor until the scraps of wood chips blended together.

Ghost coaxed her, wishing he could say the perfect thing to make her smile. "How could you ever turn out like the Landlord?"

"It's not that difficult to imagine. Being trapped in this building forever because I don't know what's going to come after me in the hallways if they find out I'm human." She pushed a bit of sawdust gingerly with her finger and began to write out her own initials.

"Do you really think any of us would let anything in this building get you?"

Dory did not answer. Instead, she picked up a little sawdust and sprinkled it back onto the floor like a child in a sandbox. Sitting down the floor next to her, Ghost attempted to nudge her with this shoulder, but his shoulder went directly through. Instead, he said, "It hasn't been all bad has it."

She couldn't help smiling. "No. It hasn't been all bad." Facing Ghost, Dory whispered, "At least I do get out. I'd hate to think of sticking around in one apartment and having to lie all the time."

Ghost pointed back at the workbench where the Landlord was stooped over something intently. "You'd need to be an expert at lying, like him."

Wrinkling her nose, Dory answered, "I think I'd have to be practicing 'till I was as old as him to be that good." She offered a smirk to Ghost who returned with a cross eyed expression, hoping to grow her smile.

Winston and Raleigh returned. "Where's the old dude?" Raleigh disrespectfully asked pointing towards the work table.

They turned in time to notice the open window. The

Landlord was gone, escaped out of a window down a homemade fire escape constructed of plastic piping and rope which instantly collapsed after he was finished using it. He left behind a change of address postcard on his desk and a note reading, "I do believe I have worn out my welcome. Take care of everyone in the building for me."

The Marley knocker's voice strained over the silence. "What's happened? Where did he go?"

"He's moved away," Dory explained to the knocker.

The voice inquired, "Really? Now why would he do that?"

Chapter Eighteen:
The Fourteenth Floor; Away to the Roof

The night was spent in the Landlord's apartment. Each member of the company rested in the respective rooms, mulling over their adventures. Winston stayed up late, practicing his own transformation with the door locked. Like a teenager practicing the asking out of his first date, he spent hours in front of the mirror while his fur grew and retracted at will. Raleigh had a heart to heart chat with the ceiling, hoping that wherever she was Georgiana could hear him. He told her about how he was trying to do what she told him, to stay safe and to become the caring man she once thought him to be. Ghost imagined where he would go first with his new found freedom to haunt and who his first targets would be. Every now and again, the edges of his mind would linger to the words of the imp and he would dare himself to also wonder about a new life within a possessed body could hold. Dory thought about the three of them, how strange it was to worry and be worried about by monsters and legends when she could not manage to stay in touch with her oldest friends. And Frank, in the true tradition of any house pet, thought about bacon.

The Marley knocker provided them with dinner and breakfast, but seemed very put out by the disappearance of his employer. They slept and changed back into their old clothes which had been cleaned and ironed.

Ghost came out from his room after the others had eaten with a happy expression as they prepared to leave.

"Look! Look everyone!" He was translucent with the green walls obviously visible through him. He leaned over Dory and grasped a lock of her hair. Feeling more triumph, he gathered more and more of her brown locks until he twisted them into two pigtails. "See!"

Oblivious to the significance of this action, Winston gave a forced, "Oh. That's nice?" He was fully human upon this morning, back to his burly yet conservative self.

Raleigh added with the same confusion and lack of enthusiasm, "Wow, she looks good."

With a happy laugh, Dory clarified, "Not the hair. He can move stuff at will while he's see-through."

"I couldn't do that before," he stated with elation and released Dory's tresses. He then concentrated on Raleigh's shirt and was able to pinch the sleeve.

The vampire edged away. "I'm glad for you and all, but be careful. This is an expensive shirt. Come on, let's get going. We have a long walk ahead of us."

Shaking her hair back out, Dory told the others she would join them in a second as they filed out of the apartment. Dory was about to hang the vintage dress back in the cupboard in the sitting room when the Marley knocker spoke up. "Eh, take it with you. It's not like I have anything to do with it."

Running her hand over the lovely material, Dory shook her head. "I really can't be carrying it all over the place."

"There is a bag at the bottom of the cupboard. Take that." The voice was trying to hide the kindness there, determined to hold onto his annoyance over his master's trickery.

"Thank you," she said with sincerity. She found a canvas satchel stashed at the back of the closet. She stuffed the dress into the satchel and was thankful to have someplace to carry the imp helmet for when the time came to use it again. She leaned down and checked the laces on her red high tops. Feeling that she was ready to start their journey again, she called up to the knocker, "Thanks for everything. What happens to you now?"

"I wait for another landlord to come," he explained, "and hope that he or she is more honest than the man previously served."

"I wish you good luck with that," Dory answered as she shifted the bag's strap. "Goodbye, Marley knocker."

"Goodbye, human woman."

The vampire, werewolf, and ghost waited outside of the apartment door for her. The metal sheeting for Raleigh's apartment and the steel cage for Winston's home were both waiting in the hallway. They couldn't help speculating what sort of creatures the maintenance men must have been. If they were humans, the Landlord wouldn't have had the knocker relay messages to them.

Moving over to the young woman while the others inspected their gifts, Ghost reached out for Dory's hand. At first her face lit up at his approach and she caught herself in the act of that happy, flustered feeling that came with a sped up heart. Her fingers twitched, as if wincing away from his chilly touch. "You okay?" he asked trying to read her expression.

She took a sidestep away from him. "No. There are a few things bothering me."

"Like?"

"Fine. All of it is bothering me," she confessed with a mournful gaze at the dark hall. "You know, there have been times over the last few days when I've wondered if this was all just a bad dream. Maybe I hit my head in the storm at my old apartment. For all I know, I'm lying unconscious in the basement surrounded by strangers!"

"Hey, calm down." Ghost managed to catch her palm in his and a chill ran up her arm. "If this is a dream, how do you explain all of us?"

"My subconscious using an image from a child's book to create a dream world I can stay in while I'm possibly dying in a coma." Dory wiggled her fingers nervously in the almost non-corporal hand.

Ghost glanced over at Winston and Raleigh who were comparing fangs with their mouths wide open and their tongues wagging side to side. "Your subconscious is messed up then."

She pulled away from him and tried to smile. "I really shouldn't hold your hand," she concluded with a sad expression, staring straight ahead down the empty hallway.

"Too cold?" he asked looking down at his own hand, questioning if he felt like cool air or if there was any substance to his touch.

"It's not that," she muttered. Dory stole a lengthy look at Ghost.

Winston and Raleigh were both obviously handsome in their own way. With his dark complexion, chiseled features, and stylish fashion, the vampire was like a classic actor, the essence of good looks. Winston had a high school football star meets all American shy boy appearance to him. If he ever left the apartment building he would have a harem of girls after him.

Then there was Ghost with his gawky, thin body and messy straw colored hair. He wasn't handsome, not in the traditional sense, but he had the nicest smile out of the three of them. Quickly, she reminded herself of two things. First, that if they made it to the top floor, she'd be gone soon. And second, Ghost was dead. Dory suddenly blushed and looked away.

"Dory?" he prodded, not noticing her embarrassment.

The young woman muttered as she avoided eye contact with the spirit, "Boy, the sooner I get home, the better." Ghost's expression went from inquisitive to a twinge of sorrow.

Winston bounded over to them. "What are we talking about?" he inquired, noticing how Dory stared at her shoes. He tried to catch her eyes, and then pulled on her arm. "What's with you?"

"Nothing. I'm fine," she grumbled with annoyance and crossed the hallway to stand with Raleigh. "Are we all ready? I'll call the imps." She noticed Raleigh wink at her as she dug through the canvas bag. "What?"

He rocked on his heels, his expression a mixture of accepted defeat and mischievous teasing. He whispered to her, his fanged mouth nearly pressing against her ear, "At least now I know why you don't fall for any of my charming vampire ways. Pity." He paused and looked at Ghost who was distractedly watching them. His grin widening, the vampire added, "Oh, look. We're making him jealous. Let's make out. Then he'll get really mad and maybe he'll finally be that scary spirit he so wants to be."

"Shut up, Raleigh!" Dory pulled on the Celtic helmet and called for the imps. They flew to the tenth floor with in seconds.

"Good morning, Miss Dory," the main imp greeted. He clicked the tops of his wings together as he bowed. "And what mischief do you have for us today?" Frank began to dance, wanting desperately for one of the imps to fly close enough for him to chase.

Dory politely asked, "Imps, is there any way you can take us to the top floor?" She really did not want to make any mischievous spirits angry with her, even if they were technically under her control for the time being.

Floating overhead like fireflies, the imps buzzed and chattered over the question. "Bor-ing request! Besides, we can only take you as far as the stairway to the fourteenth floor," the main imp told her. "Gilda will not permit us beyond that point."

Winston groaned and slapped a heavy hand over his

own face. "You mean she has powers too? Not more magic."

"Well, I do not actually know about powers. She asked us very kindly not pass the fourteenth floor and gave us a fruit basket. We can respect people who are respectful." The other imps began to snicker and the main imp added, "Okay, most times that is not true, but in this case we have made an exception."

"So, you're technically doing something tricky to be bringing us that close," Dory pointed out. "Not as boring as you thought, right?"

The imp struggled with this. He twisted his fingers around the edges of his wings. "Oh, alright," he conceded. "Not like we can refuse you when you're wearing the helmet anyway."

The imps lifted the four into the air again. They flew them up each staircase, through the dark hallways, and dropped them un-ceremonially at the landing of the fourteenth floor. Dory thanked the imp again. The main imp grunted in response, but was secretly pleased with the praise.

Chapter Nineteen:
The Fourteenth Floor; Attacked by the Annoyed Mummies

The imps dropped them off in the middle of the fourteenth floor, then flew away giggling like naughty children. Instead of doors, the fourteenth floor was lined with fancy, ancient coffins all propped up. Faces were painted upon each, wearing gold crowns and holding important looking scepters.

Ghost turned back to look down the stairway, then at the hallway of the fourteenth floor once again. "Did I miss something? When did we go on a field trip?"

"They're Egyptian, aren't they," Winston stated. He stood perfectly in the middle of the corridor. He wanted to be as far from the rows of the Egyptian coffins as he could.

"A sarcophagus," Raleigh corrected. He moved over to one of the standing coffins and slapping his hand against the elaborately painted wood. "This, my friend, is called a sarcophagus."

Winston gulped, made nervous by Raleigh's close proximity to the box. "But there is a dead person in there right?"

"Technically there's a dead person next to it too," Ghost pointed out.

Raleigh, ignoring Ghost's comment, answered Winston's question, "You betcha!" Holding open the sarcophagus so all could see the brown bandaged corpse, Raleigh teased, "Hey, Ghost, found a new body for you."

"Mummies?" Ghost asked with confusion.

Winston wrung his hands. "Run! Let's run! Right now! I've seen this movie."

Raleigh scoffed and replaced the sarcophagus lid, "Okay, despite what Hollywood tells you, I have never ever heard of a mummy attacking or cursing anyone. They're probably just here because some Egyptologist stashed them."

"Grave robbers?" Ghost restated. "Just what we need."

"They aren't grave robbers," Dory corrected, "They're historians."

The vampire scoffed. "If they move dead human beings from their resting place and hide them in an apartment building, they're grave robbers."

She then pointed at Raleigh with warning, "And as for Hollywood being wrong, I always assumed they and books made up vampires, ghosts, werewolves, headless horsemen, sirens, ghouls, imps—"

"You didn't know what imps were before we saw them yesterday," Ghost corrected.

"It doesn't matter. You're missing the point," she ranted.

"You have a point?" Raleigh grumbled.

"The point is that if those mummies come to life and kill us or curse us or do anything else that they shouldn't be doing because they're dead, I'm blaming all of you!"

"Why?" Winston squeaked.

"Because you all keep telling me that it's safe or that you have it under control and then something jumps out at us." She lifted up Frank and shot up her chin. "You all need to work on saying that you were wrong every once in a while." With that she started down the hallway with all of the confidence and manner of a woman exasperated.

As if they heard her, each of the sarcophagi burst

open. The lids fell to the floor, some sliding several feet away. One hit Winston in the leg and Raleigh instantly leaped over another lid as he moved away from the mummy he had been taunting.

"Ha! Wrong again, Mr. Vampire!" Dory shouted. Her triumph quickly ebbed as panic fell upon her. The mummies each held out their arms in front, the sound of their old wrapping crunching as they moved. Dory cowered a little to the middle of the hallway. "Oh crap."

As the mummies stumbled forward blindly, their faces covered by wrappings, they began to wave their padded arms. With immense force, Dory was knocked to the ground. The others each took a defensive stand. A total of six mummies wandered up and down the hallway. When they bumped walls, they left dents in the wood.

A mummy trudged towards them and slapped Raleigh in the face. Ghost dodged another bandaged arm and wondered out loud, "Why would anyone put mummies to work as guardians?"

Winston instantly suggested, "Maybe the daddies are having trouble finding work."

Raleigh groaned. "Oh, just let the mummies kill him, please!"

Winston growled and partially transformed into the wolf as another mummy attempted to bat him upside the face. His head and upper body slouched, growing fur while his legs remained human. He sunk his teeth into one of the ancient arms and then spit onto the ground in disgust.

Ghost turned invisible and moved over to Dory. She and Frank were attempting to crawl towards the stairs, ducking under the mummy arms. "How you holding up?" his disembodied voice asked her.

"I'm very annoyed at Raleigh right now and this floor is gross. But other than that just dandy." She sat for a moment and began to slam her fist onto mummy feet like she was playing a whack-a-mole game.

With a sigh, Ghost answered, "Okay, sit tight or follow my lead if you want. I might have an idea."

She looked in the direction of his voice. "Why are you invisible? They can't see anything' they're eyes are bandaged."

"Well, Winston was using his power and Raleigh is all fangs and scariness. I just wanted to do something supernatural too," he explained trying to hide the pout in his voice.

Dory tried not to sound tired as she answered, "Oh. That makes sense."

Ghost came back into view, and then ran up behind one of the mummies. "Raleigh, Winston," he shouted at them, "Bumper cars!" He yelled the words with such conviction, one would've thought he'd announced the charge of a cavalry.

Dory understood instantly. She jumped up and stood behind another mummy. Both she and Ghost tapped the mummies on the shoulders, and then jumped in front of them. "Follow us," they both taunted. The ghost and girl backed into one another, then quietly as possible, sunk to the ground and crawled out of the paths of the two mummies. The mummies collided, the force scattering both walking corpses so they lay on the floor. Their legs and arms had broken off and their bandages were jarred revealing the embalmed, pickled flesh beneath.

Raleigh did the same, insulting his mummy as it followed him. "Come on, you walking fourth grade prank. Remind me to call you next time I run out of toilet paper." The mummy reached out, swinging its arms in a scissor motion across the front of his chest. Winston and Raleigh ducked at that moment, causing the mummy's arms to cut across a second mummy. Once again they landed in a pile of body parts on the floor.

Ghost and Raleigh took care of the last pair in the same manner. The group surveyed their handiwork with pride. "We made a mess," Winston pointed out as he kicked at the thousands of years of Egyptian dust scattering the floor.

"We also destroyed priceless artifacts," Dory added with sadness.

"Better than being hugged to death by Boris Karloff," Raleigh pointed out.

Pulling at his yellow hair with confusion, Ghost stated, "I thought Karloff was the Frankenstein monster."

"He was both," Raleigh explained. Just then he noticed a mummy hand in the heap begin to twitch. "Uh oh!"

All twelve severed hands started to dig their fingers into the floor in attempt to pull themselves towards the travelers. The feet started to hop without any legs to support them. The heads wriggled back and forth in an odd scooting motion. The appendages moved towards them with surprising speed. Frank began to paw and growl as a single toe shuffled by him.

"Run!" Winston declared in a high pitched scream. He led the way up the stairs as the others tripped over each other and Frank in order to escape the crawling mummy fingers.

As they arrived at the landing at the top of the stairs, Dory eyed Raleigh and pursed her lips. "What do we say?" she asked him like a berating mother.

He shrugged and told her, "Okay, I was wrong." She gave him a little glare and he quickly added, "I'm sorry?" His voice was thick with stubbornness.

Ghost chuckled. "Apologize better than that or we're never going to hear the end of it."

With a sigh, Raleigh repeated with sincerity, "I'm sorry."

The joyful feeling of being right filling her with energy,

Dory jumped to her feet. "That's better. I think I'm ready for the next floor now."

All of the men gave each other exhausted expressions, then struggled to their feet and followed the young woman to the fifteenth floor.

Chapter Twenty:
The Fifteenth Floor; The Shambling Zombie Home

The fifteenth floor appeared to have only one apartment on it, just like the Landlord's floor. The single door showed no signs of life. They could hear no voices behind it or any feet pacing the floor.

"We only have to get by one door," Winston cried out. "This is great! Let's go!"

The door seemed to hear him and instantly swung open. "Now you've done it," Raleigh moaned.

Voices called out from the darkness of the apartment, each one coming out in a drawn-out, lost groan. Yet, through the mumbling, the group could make out a single word. "Brrrrrraaaaaaaiiiiiiinnnnnnnsssss."

A gust of strong, rancid wind entered the hallway. The four people and the little dog were blown every which way. They dug their feet into the floor, yet one by one they were pulled into the apartment.

They landed in a pile at the middle of the room with poor Winston at the bottom. Dory was the first up. The space before them was unlit and unkempt. She could see half a dozen pairs of eyes staring her down, the eyes catching the light from the hallway like cats in the dark. The eyes started to shift and move slowly.

Raleigh and Ghost helped Winston to his feet. Frank began to bark loudly at the moaned word "Braaaaains!" Men and women came into the light, each of them rotting further with every step. Their discolored skin hung off of them like baggy clothing. Some had limbs missing; others had body parts hanging by a thread. One man even had an eye dangling from the socket, the rubber ball hanging from the end of the paddle. Only their teeth appeared to be intact, a mouth full of them surrounded by dried blood mustaches.

"Zombies," Dory squeaked, "I though Hollywood made those up too!"

"Actually, zombies come from the voodoo religion. Hollywood just dressed it up," Ghost explained.

Raleigh bared his fangs at the approaching corpses. "No offense, Ghost, but not caring about the history lesson right now."

Winston edged against the others as they formed a circle. They kept their backs to one another and their eyes on the stumbling zombies. "I wouldn't mind a little history. Do they really eat brains?"

The zombies edged closer, one of them reaching out her hand and swatting at the air in front of her as if she were swimming through oxygen. "Brains!" she cried out.

The other five zombies answered like a war cry in unison, "Braaains!"

"What do you think?" Raleigh answered. "Ghost will be okay. He doesn't actually have a body, even in solid form you don't really have any brains to eat."

"Oh, so I just get to watch you all get eaten. Thanks," Ghost grumbled. "What are we going to do?!" He thought for a long moment. "If we only had some brains," he murmured as the others all gave him a confused expression. "You know, like extra brains to throw at them or something."

Dory lightly kicked Frank to the center of their circle, not certain if zombies were partial to dog brains. "Could we somehow lead them down to the ghoul? This looks like a feast for him."

"I don't think we could make it that many floors down," Ghost pointed out. "What we need is a mall to hide in. Or a big scary werewolf, what do you say, Winston."

The man was wringing his hands and whimpered, "Can't transform. Already tried. Too scared. Childhood nightmares about zombies."

Raleigh groaned, "Oh great. Winston's not here right now, but if you'd like to leave a message wait for the scream of terror." He pushed Winston's shoulder to make certain the werewolf was at least responsive. Winston jumped at Raleigh's touch. The vampire nodded. "Okay, I say we run for the door on the count of three. One. Two. Three!"

Dory picked up Frank and was last in the line of sprinters. Winston was first, booking it to the door as if a zombie were right on his tail. They could still hear the chorus of "Brains!" Each one of them glanced back over their shoulders in dread. They watched the zombies shuffle towards them. Their panic subsided and their running slowed.

"They're barely moving at all," Ghost pointed out.

Raleigh laughed heartily. "Hey, check out the short bus candidates of the occult world."

Dory flicked the vampire behind the ear and he hissed in annoyance. "Raleigh, you're being insensitive again. If you keep saying awful, discriminating things, I'm giving you a sunbath," she scolded. She watched as one of the zombies arms flit limply back and forth at its side like cooked pasta. "They are pretty funny though," she added with a wide smile.

"Then let's just get out of here," Winston pleaded. "We've seen the show; let's go before we're dinner."

The group turned away and sauntered to back to the door without panic. Dory was still last in line. She set down Frank who ran ahead of them all to be back in the safety of the hallway.

A seventh zombie none of them had noticed before ambled out of the darkness near the entrance. He was missing an ear and had to flinch his shoulder repeatedly in order to make the muscles in his arm work. Tripping on his own feet, the zombie landed near the door and grabbed Dory's foot as she passed by. She saw the walls spiral away until the ceiling came into view and felt a sharp pain against her head. The last thing she heard as the world went black was, "Braaaaains!"

When she opened her eyes again, Dory lay on the hallway floor. Winston's shirt was rolled up under her head. Blood had dried in her hair, sticking to her forehead and staining her cheek. She looked up at the three men staring down at her with worried smiles.

"What happened?" she murmured. "Why am I on the floor? Where's Frank?" Upon hearing his name, the little dog let out a yip from where he was in Winston's arms.

Raleigh explained, "Zombie attack. We pulled you out of the room, but one of them grabbed your foot."

"Don't tell me I was bitten by one of those walking rag dolls?" Dory complained thinking how embarrassing it would be to make it passed spiders and mummies only to be taken down by one the slowest moving monster of all time.

"No, you weren't bitten," Winston added, wanting to be helpful. "You hit your head on the door frame."

Dory tried to turn her head to hide her face. "Still embarrassing," she muttered.

Ghost, with more understanding of the situation, ran his fingers over her eyebrows and pulled upward gently for a better look at her pupils. "You should have a concussion. I'm amazed that you don't. And you might need stitches."

Dory's gaze darted from Ghost at the frightening sound of medical procedures. Winston was holding the little dog. He moved Frank close to her to give the squirming puppy a chance to lick her hand.

She said with amazement, "You can be that close to Frank? You aren't wolfing out."

"No, I guess I'm not," Winston answered, scratching Frank behind the ear. He retrieved his shirt from the floor and pulled it on.

"You hit your head pretty hard," Raleigh explained. "Luckily, Ghost here acted quickly. He had us clean you up and he checked you for a concussion and he even made sure that zombie who grabbed you didn't scratch your leg. He named off all of these antibiotics we could try finding if you had an infection." He leaned down, adding in a whisper, "He kept rambling. That's the stuff I could understand."

She reached up and brushed her hand against the dried blood, a little of it flaking onto her finger. "Raleigh, are you doing okay? You aren't going to try to bite me again, are you?"

"No, no," he assured her. "I don't feel any urge to feed right now."

Lastly, she looked up at Ghost. "You knew what to do?"

"I remembered something from being alive," he quietly answered, "I was a medical student. I used to study how to help people when they were hurt or scared." He ran his cool hand over her wound to check for a fever or any further bleeding. "I still don't remember anything else, though."

"No. That's good, Ghost," she encouragingly told him. Her face ached as she smiled. "In fact, that's awesome." She smiled at all three of them and added, "At the risk of sounding cheesy, I'm really proud of all three of you." Frank made a curious little whine and Dory added, "Yes, Frank. I'm proud of you too."

Setting his hand on her arm, Ghost smiled, "This is all great. Love the bonding and all, but you need a doctor, a real doctor. Someone who can look at that cut and take care of it."

"But we've come too far to give up now," Dory argued. She sat up and the room spun around her. She attempted to cover up her dizziness with more talk. "Besides, how could you three take me to a doctor? It's daylight. Ghost, you can't leave the building. And Winston, you *won't* leave the building."

His bottom lip quivering a little with a shyness he had not shown in several days, Winston murmured, "I would've left the building to take you to the doctor."

Despite Ghost's protests, Dory allowed Raleigh to help her up off the floor. She leaned between him and Winston while announcing, "Okay, off we go."

As they started towards the stairs, Winston nudged Dory. "Were you really proud of me back there?"

She nodded and answered through closed lips. "Mmm hmm."

"I've never had a woman be proud of me before except my mom," Winston admitted. Raleigh snickered but the others ignored it.

"Moms count," Dory told him with sympathy.

"Not in the same way though," the werewolf explained sheepishly.

Raleigh watched Ghost grumble to himself about safety and concussions as he walked ahead of the group. "Dory, you better go talk to him. He's not paying attention; he's going to end up walking straight through a wall."

Dory nodded and released both of the arms holding her up and swayed carefully over to Ghost. Winston gave Raleigh a death glare for sending her up to walk with the spirit when she had been so comfortably balanced on his arm. The vampire just gave him a pitying expression and hissed, "Forget it, buddy, we already lost that fight."

When Dory and Ghost were a little ahead of the group, she pointed out to him, "If I was dying, you could have done the body transplant thing like the imp said. I mean . . . I don't completely get how it works, but if I'm already slipping away and there . . . if there is no hope. You can always—"

They started up the stairs, Dory gripped tightly to the rail thanks to her head injury. Ghost smiled at her and offered a hand if she needed it. "Dory, first of all, I wouldn't take over your body no matter what. Unless I am under the influence of another imp, that is. Second, I couldn't constantly know that I was alive while you never had a second chance. Plus, I'd be too scared that the body that would form around me would be a girl forever."

Sticking out her tongue at him, Dory nodded. "Good point. You'd make a lousy woman."

Raleigh moved between them. "What are we talking about?"

"Ghost with boobs," Dory stated nonchalantly.

Raleigh instantly froze. "Um, lifestyle change? Not that I'm judging. You go, dude. Do what feels right." The words were tight between his lips. He gave Dory a silent plea not to throw him out into the sunlight. *"See, I'm supportive,"* his eyes tried to say.

"It's not a lifestyle anything, Raleigh," Ghost said. "We were just joking around about something."

"Hey, I'm all for the idea of you possessing some unsuspecting person and having a second life," Raleigh dispassionately told them.

Ghost, Winston, and Dory all gaped at the vampire. "That's the second time you brought that up. The imp told us about it, but you knew?" Dory asked almost shaking. "Raleigh, you honestly are pushing for Ghost to possess someone?"

Winston threw his hands in the air. "I really don't think I want to know what we're talking about."

The vampire rotated his shoulders and squared his stance. "I've heard the stories of people killed before their time becoming ghosts and that's about it. There aren't exact guidelines for these things, you know. And it isn't like we've seen any dying people for him to take over. But the fact is, Ghost, that someday you might have the chance. I just want you to be able to take it."

Winston asked with interest, "Would the zombie count as a dying body?"

Raleigh made a face. "No. A zombie counts as a disgusting, rotting corpse. Not suitable for possession by a ghost."

Ghost added, "Really, I'm not in a hurry to try that out. I can't really imagine living in someone else's body."

"I hear it becomes your body though," Raleigh told him. "Especially if you've been dead long enough for few people to recognize you. You were probably a good guy in life. It's not right that you didn't get to live it."

With a sigh, Ghost determinedly decided, "Thanks, but no thanks. I don't think I could do it."

Raleigh shook his head, "Suit yourself." He then whispered to Dory, "Just trying to help." She replied by taking a step back and stomping on his toe.

Chapter Twenty-One:
    The Sixteenth Floor; The Werewolf Becomes the
    Leader of a Support Group

They arrived on the sixteenth floor only find that that it was barred. Someone had constructed a metal security gate over the front of the hallway, blocking their way.

Dory rattled the gate. "That's pretty strong. Anyone know how to pick locks?"

"I might," Ghost offered, feeling confident from the little bit of information about his own past he had been able to remember. "But I might know a lot of things I just can't completely remember."

Winston sniffed the air. "Wait. Dory, get away from that door."

"Why?" As she asked, three werewolves pounced upon the other side of the security gate. They snarled and spat at them through the bars. Dory jumped backwards as Raleigh hissed.

Winston picked up Frank and pet the little dog for a minute, watching the three monsters growling from within the hallway. Setting the puppy back down, Winston transformed once again into his wolf form. He pounced at the security door and snarled back at the three opponents.

The werewolves yelped and backed away at Winston's barks. Cowering as they escaped into one of the apartments, they slowly transformed back into humans. Two teenage boys and a young girl vanished into the apartment and slammed the door.

Winston returned to his human self. "That was weird," he commented, then banged on the security door. "Hey! Hey, you three. Let us in!"

Dory and Raleigh watched Winston with an impressed nod of their heads. Ghost whispered, "Is he being forceful? Is Winston actually taking charge?"

"Shh," Raleigh whispered. "Don't say anything or you'll jinx it. I'm really sick of dealing with the whiny side of him."

"I can hear you," Winston groaned, but kept his eyes on the apartment door where the young werewolves had gone.

Raleigh gritted his teeth. "Oops, sorry, buddy. You know I don't have the highest patience level."

Winston was too busy dealing with the fearful young werewolves. "Come on out. I don't bite. I want to talk. I'm just like you."

After a while, the apartment door opened. The little girl stepped out. Her blonde hair was an uneven mess like she had once tried to trim it herself. She wore tattered shorts and a holey pink princess tee-shirt. She carried a Barbie under her arm. The doll was missing a leg and wore Kleenex as a dress.

She stood on the other side of the security door, staring out at Winston. "My brothers don't want me to let you in," she told them. "But I'm going to let you. Only you have to promise not eat us or try to fight us or anything like that."

"I promise," Winston told her, studying her plump little hand and dirty fingernails as it reached for the lock on the security door.

"What about them?" she asked her hand inches from the lock. Ghost offered the girl a smile and Raleigh rolled his eyes.

"We promise too," Dory told her.

The door was opened and the little girl took Dory's hand. "My brothers are scared of all of you," she explained, "so let's go in quietly."

Winston walked directly behind them in line. Raleigh was third. Ghost and Frank were the last to enter the apartment where the girl's brothers had taken refuge. Beside the two teen wolves, there were four women and three other men. Some were partially transformed, with pointed wolf ears sticking to the sides of their heads or tails twitching behind them.

"What is this place?" Winston wanted to know as the three of the werewolves morphed back into full humans.

"This is our sanctuary," one of the male wolves said as his nose shortened and his teeth retracted to normal.

The room was a mess with take-out packages and pizza boxes lining the walls where furniture should have been. Raleigh took a step forward and a chicken bone crunched under his foot. Winston's stomach turned at the sight of dirty clothes collecting mold in a corner and flies buzzing over the remnants of rotting food. The werewolf swayed a little from the smell.

"Sanctuary? You never leave here do you," Winston repeated. "You're all . . . all like me. A horribly, frighteningly messy me."

"You're a werewolf?" one of the women asked looking mournful at her own fate.

"Yes, but I was talking about the bars on the hallway," Winston pointed out. "You don't get out much, do you?"

One of the male wolves explained, "This is where we can talk about our troubles with others just like us. Why would we leave the safety of others who know what we're going through?"

"It's a werewolf support group," Dory restated with a stunned, "Huh."

"I used to go to things like this when I was breaking

the habit of human blood," Raleigh pointed out. Three werewolves looked at him with terror. "Yeah. I'm vampire. Get over it."

One of the men snarled. Raleigh glared at him and the man instantly shrunk into his seat. Winston covered a snicker and muttered, "Tell me I'm not this bad."

Raleigh went to open his mouth, but Dory stomped on his foot to stop him from making a rude comment. She then walked over to Winston, nudging him towards the skittish werewolves. "Maybe you should talk to them. Tell them about what it was like to leave your apartment. You might want to downplay some of the dangerous stuff though."

"Oh, right," Winston said. He cleared his throat and caught the attention of the various people in the room. "You all need to learn to better control your powers. Don't be so afraid of what you are and stop hiding from the world."

The little girl was the only one to respond. The others stared at Winston as if he had just spoken to them in an alien tongue. "Do you go outside?"

"I'm working on it?" he answered truthfully.

"I want to go outside," she quietly admitted. "I want to go the park."

"How long have you all been here?" Ghost wanted to know.

"About a year," one of the girl's brothers explained. "We were on a tour bus of Germany, but our guide turned out to be—" He hung his head and rubbed his arm as if there were a wound there only he could see.

"He bit us all," the little girl finished without sadness or fear. "We all decided to stick together since then."

Winston nodded with understanding. "I was bit a long time ago, but I was all by myself." He leaned down to look at the little girl's round face. He could see dark circles under her eyes and he thought of the school she missed, friends she never saw, and the important growing up she lacked while hiding in the apartment. "You really want to go to the park?"

"Yeah," she whispered. Her eyes widened. "I want to go on the swing."

"Okay." Winston smiled at her with complete resolve. "On Monday, we go to the park." He stood up tall and said to the others, "In fact, on Monday, let's all go to the park."

A man jumped from his chair and waved his hands in protest. "No! Oh no! We can't go outside. Things trigger it. We go outside, we eat birds and bunnies and . . . other things."

Setting a reassuring hand on the little girl's shoulder, Winston promised, "I won't let you. Let's consider this an experiment. We can all go outside together and we can work on not letting our transformations get the better of us. If any of us feel like we're slipping, we can come back inside."

"There's a park right across the street," Dory offered. "I saw it when I was out for a run. It's close enough that if you feel like you're changing you can run inside."

"Can we go today?" the little girl asked with hope.

"Not today. I have to help my other friend first," Winston explained gently. "I'll be back." He faced the other werewolves. "What do you say?"

There was a great deal of deliberation between the group of frightened people. They huddled with the little girl in the middle. Ghost and Raleigh both tried to listen in, but one of the female werewolves dared a dark look that made them back off. It was four or five minutes before their think tank dispersed.

One of the women acted as the representative for the group. "We miss going outside," she confessed. "We'll go to the park with you, but if anything bad happens to any one of us, the rest will kill you."

Winston knitted his eyebrows. "That's . . . extreme," he answered. "Okay, deal. I'll be here at noon on Monday. And perhaps we can turn this into a regular meeting. We can keep trying new places and staying outside longer."

"Let's just start with the park," the woman told him doubtfully.

"We'll start with the park," Winston answered, nodding his head with enthusiasm. "And now we have to go, but I'll be back." He directed his attention once more to the little girl. "See you on Monday."

She smiled at him, her eyes twinkling. "I'll let you guys out of the gate," she offered. She grabbed Winston's hand and led them to the security gate at the other end of the hallway separating them from the upward stairs. She unlocked the deadbolt. Dory, Ghost, and Raleigh walked through first. Dory waved at the little girl who was reluctant to release Winston's hand. "Monday, don't forget."

He squeezed her fingers in his and grinned. "I won't be late."

Joining his friends, Winston looked back at the child watching them from the security gate as they started up the stairs. "Did I do the right thing?" he asked the others, "or do you think I should just let them stay as they are?"

"Were you really happy when you never left your apartment?" Dory reasoned.

Winston thought it over for a second. "No," he admitted with defeat.

Raleigh challenged, "How happy have you been out here with us?"

"Are you kidding? It's been terrifying," Winston confessed. "I'm scared of everything and all I've wanted to do the whole time is run back to my apartment to hide under the bed."

"But are you happy?" Raleigh asked.

"Despite the scary stuff, I'm glad I came. I'm having fun," Winston told them.

"Then you did the right thing," Dory stated. "And you took charge. That was pretty impressive."

Winston's head tilted back with pride. "Yeah. And you know what? I'm really looking forward to helping them. Does anyone want to come with the park with us on Monday?"

Everyone hesitated, thinking of the many worried werewolves huddling under the jungle gym to hide from someone's dog. "We'll consider it," Ghost at last answered on behalf of the group, despite the fact that he couldn't leave the building.

Chapter Twenty-Two:
     The Seventeenth Floor; The Apartment of the Rejected
     Science Projects

The seventeenth floor was a short hallway, with one poorly constructed door sitting lonely amongst a brown wall. They walked to the end of the hallway, discovering nothing but a dead end.

"What do we do now?" Dory mournfully asked, leaning against the wall, "There's no more stairs."

Ghost pointed to the only door. "Maybe the Landlord was wrong. What if Gilda lives on the seventeenth floor."

Raleigh rotated his shoulders with a readied stance. "Only one way to find out," he said and knocked three times on the wood.

"Come in," a voice called back.

Raleigh glanced at the others, and then was the first to walk into the apartment. Winston, Ghost, and Frank entered next. Dory was the last to go in but what she saw made her jump three feet into the air.

The room was full of men and women who all had stitches across their skin holding them together. Bolts came out from the sides of their necks and they wore tight hospital patient robes. They had dolls and action figures strewn around the room. One was even stacking wooden blocks and another was sitting on a broken rocking horse, crying that the toy had buckled under his weight.

"What is this?" Dory murmured, her heart going out to the horrifying creatures, "They look like—"

"Like Frankenstein's creature," Raleigh finished for her. "We should move through here quickly."

"Where are the stairs?" Ghost asked.

"Over that way," one of the Frankenstein creatures answered pointing at a corner across the room. "Right around there. They go up to the nice lady's place." The great monsters spoke like children, some of their voices high pitched, others pouted.

"Great," Raleigh grumbled, "Let's get out of this butcher shop."

Suddenly one of the creatures stood to full height and roared at them. "Settle down," Dory heard herself shout. "He didn't mean it!" The creature looked curious, and then dropped his arms which he had raised over his head menacingly and sat back down on the floor. He picked up a Raggedy Andy doll and pretended it was walking along the baseboard of the wall.

"You must be very, very kind to us or we go on monstrous rampages," the female creature explained with the simplicity of a child.

"We need to feel loved," another of the creature told them nodding his head, but keeping his eyes on his coloring book.

Raleigh leaned down over them. "Okay then, we really appreciate you telling us where to go next. Now promise not to rampage?"

"We promise," another creature, with Asian facial features, but wiry black hair that domed over the top of his head like a baby bonnet. "But what about the master?"

"The master?" Dory repeated with a gulp.

"Yes," a man's voice called out, "the master!" Everyone turned as a man in a white lab coat stepped out from amongst the many childlike creations. He had a thin mustache and slicked back black hair. "Excellent," he announced, clapping his gloved hands together. "New parts!" He then turned to the many monsters. "My little children, we have new brothers and a sister for you. Make certain they do not leave you."

All of the Frankenstein creatures rose from the floor, abandoning their toys and books to stretch out their arms towards the travelers. They looked like toddlers begging to be lifted into the air and cuddled. With the strength of metal cranes, each of the creatures gabbed for the four and hugged them tightly into place.

Ghost tried to turn invisible, but a male creature already had him within his grasp. He was too solid and too panicked to try any of his other abilities. Winston transformed, but the sight of the werewolf did not phase the scientist and his minions. He thrashed and growled, but they held him tight. Raleigh bared his teeth and hissed loudly, but one of the creatures simply clamped his mouth shut with annoyance.

A smaller of the Frankenstein monsters lifted up Frank and yelled, "Doggie!"

The scientist came to look over them, his thumb holding up Dory's chin to look at her with admiration, as if she were already something he had made. "Yes, yes. You shall be my greatest." He then leaned in close and whispered, "Just between you and me, these others have been quite the disappointments."

Dory instantly knew what to do at that comment. She answered, "What? What was that, sir? What did you say about disappointments?"

The man's pupils dilated and his Adam's apple quivered. "Shh!" the scientist snapped at her.

Dory wriggled her shoulders within the grip of the creature holding her. Unlike the zombies, the creatures had a sweet, earthy scent like daisies. "You heard him, didn't you? He called you a disappointment."

The creature loosened her grip on Dory. "You did say

that," she said with a puppy dog stare "You didn't mean it, did you?"

"Of course I didn't," the scientist cooed. "I love each of you dearly." He gave Dory a dark look and added, "Gag her."

As one of the creatures tied a doll dress around Dory's mouth, Raleigh spoke up, understanding what Dory was doing. "You say that, but if he's so pleased with all of you, why does he want to make more of you? What does he want us for?"

"He wants to make us more friends," the creature holding Raleigh pointed out.

"Wouldn't that take just more attention away from each of you if there are more of you?" Ghost reasoned for them. "Are any of you getting enough attention as it is?"

"You forgot my birthday yesterday!" the smaller creature holding Frank said through large tears. "You remembered Number Four's birthday last week!"

"See," Raleigh insisted. "You all deserve better than that. You deserve to be cared about, right?"

"Right," two of the creatures agreed with scowls.

The scientist took a step back. "Now, my little ones, you don't want to hurt your master."

"No," Ghost put in with a ruthless tone. "You shouldn't hurt him. In fact, why don't you each give him a great big hug?"

With excited light in their second-hand eyes, the creatures each released the travelers, descending upon their creator with their arms out ready to embrace him. He yelled for them to stay away, but still they chased him into the bedroom, calling out to him lovingly. As the last of them vanished, they could hear the scientist scream that he couldn't breathe. A moment later, they heard the heavy feet of the monsters start to shuffle back.

Dory picked up Frank and she turned to Ghost. "Turn

the lights off!"

There were a couple of sparks and the light bulbs burnt themselves out. Raleigh use his nocturnal eyes in order to be the first to leave the apartment. The four of them ran up the stairs after him and up to the eighteenth floor, wondering what sort of fiend could be guarding the door to Gilda's apartment.

Chapter Twenty-Three:
The Eighteenth Floor; Gilda Grants Dory's Wish

The stairs from within the apartment leading upwards took the group to a pair of glass French doors with bright yellow curtains behind them. The sight seemed unnatural after so much darkness within the building. A hand written sign was on the inside of the door reading in cursive "Unlocked. Come on in".

Dory turned the shiny brass handle. They entered a spacious living room decorated with comfortable white wooden furniture surrounding an elaborately painted lazy Susan table. The walls were decorated with photos from the last sixty years. The same woman was in each, doing a different fabulous activity. She was on a stage bowing before a full house. She was playing with wild beasts in a jungle somewhere. She was standing on the top of a ruin in England, a banner overhead reading "Welcome Gilda". She was in audience with the Dali Lama. She had ridden on horses, flown planes, traveled the world, and met amazing people.

A woman entered the room. She looked nothing like her age. She wore a comfortable, yet ornate dress of white silk, showing that her body was still youthful despite her number of years. Her white hair was piled atop her head like a woven basket. Hanging from her ears was a pair of delicate diamonds and resting against her neck was a ceramic rose on a chain.

"Dorothea, so you have come at last to see me," she

said with her arms spread out in a friendly manner.

Dory felt meek in the beautiful woman's presence. "You . . . you were expecting us?" she asked, staring down at the Oriental rug under her feet.

"I was, yes," Gilda explained with a graceful nod of her head. Gilda ran her fingers along the side of Dory's face like a grandmother admiring a granddaughter's growing beauty. "What is it that you want, my dear?"

At first the young woman glanced back at her companions with a nervous purse of her lips. They each offered her a warm expression and Ghost nodded at her to say what she came to say. "I want to have my lease changed. I signed on to live here for three months, not three years," Dory explained, respectfully holding out her folded up contract to the woman.

"I see," Gilda answered. She then turned to the other three who hung their heads as a sign of admiration. "And what will each of you do after Dory has left here? Winston, my dear, let us start with you."

Winston raised his eyes to meet her and he smiled wistfully. "We met some other werewolves on our way up here. They were so scared. I want to help them and help myself." He was amazed by how easy it was to answer the woman. He did not feel anxious or scared.

"That is very noble of you," she told him with a sweet smile. "You will do wonderfully at this, I promise you."

With this news, Winston grinned, yet stepped away as if he knew instinctively his conversation with the woman was done.

She looked at the vampire. "And you Raleigh? Have you found what you're looking for?"

"Maybe," Raleigh answered her honestly. He straightened his collar and fought the urge to smooth the wrinkles in his expensive shirt. "I think I'm on my way to getting what I want. I think I'll try to get to know some of the neighbors better. Maybe the more people I know, the more emotions I'll remember how to understand. And maybe I can be less of an insensitive jerk."

"That will be hard road. But you seem willing to be able to take the sour with the sweet. Your Georgiana is so proud of you," Gilda told him with a soft voice.

Raleigh's gaze instantly shot up, his eyes shining a little. "Thank you," he murmured. "Thank you for that."

Turning to Ghost, Gilda went on. "And you, young man without name or memories, what shall you do without Dory around?"

Ghost looked at Dory for a long while. He wanted to say something, but instead he turned back to Gilda and shrugged his shoulders. "I wish I had a way to start a new life," he confessed at last, "but even if I did, I wouldn't know what to do with it. I know I want to do more than just haunt. After all, I suck at it."

"Well, I am looking for a new landlord," she told him with a secretive smirk, "if you are interested? I have a feeling you would be quite a bit more trustworthy than my last employee."

Ghost beamed back at her, but did not answer.

With the lease in hand, the woman returned her attention to the girl. "Dory, follow me."

Gilda took them to the roof. A garden had been created there, fragrant and exotic, full of life. The sky was pink and orange as the horizon hid the sun. Instantly, Frank rolled up in the sunlight, peacefully taking in the warmth of the day. Dory glanced back at where the others hung in the doorway. Raleigh stayed behind Winston and Ghost, who kept his shape solid in order to block the sun's rays better.

The woman asked Dory, "Why is it that you want your contract changed?"

"I—" Suddenly, every reason Dory had seemed far away. She looked out over the city, thinking back on her long adventure. "A lot can happen in three years."

"That it can," Gilda replied. She folded her hands in front of her. "And I am aware that this is not the simplest place to live in. If you like, I can release you from your lease the moment you have a new place to live."

Dory glanced back at the men hovering in the doorway then along the rows of flowers, focusing on a purple blossom. "I just want to go home," she heard herself say without really thinking about her own words.

Gilda watched her with interest. "And where is that?"

"Downstairs," Dory said her voice full of realization. "Back to my apartment. I want to stay. I want to be here until something changes. I . . . I think I like it here." She spoke the last sentence with utter distaste and amazement, obviously surprised by her decision. Then she quickly corrected herself. "But I can't stay here forever. I can't survive living with . . . all this. I don't know. I feel a little mixed up."

With her hands clasped in front of her, Gilda tapped the folded up contract against her skirt. "I shall make you a deal, Dorothea. If you give me the helmet of the imps, I will agree to whatever lease you wish."

Digging into the bag hung across her front, Dory smiled at the woman as she gave her the iron helmet. "It's a deal!"

Gilda seemed pleased by Dory's enthusiasm. "Thank you," she said taking the helmet in her hands. "Winston, Raleigh, Ghost, I will tell the imps to take you each back to your apartments. Dory, go say your goodbyes."

"Why? Won't I see them again?" Dory asked with worry as she ran to the doorway where the men awaited her.

"That all depends on what you decide. Just because you choose to live her longer does not mean that you might not become like the other humans in this building, hidden behind a closed door and pretending that you didn't see what you just saw. Either way, it's only polite to tell a person goodbye at the end of a long day," Gilda announced.

Dory rushed to the doorway, stepping within for fear of exposing Raleigh to sunlight. The three were shuffling their feet and avoiding eye contact, each one attempting to hide his emotions by looking at the ceiling.

First, Winston held Dory at arm's length, thinking about germs. Then, he hugged Dory almost as a surrender. "Please don't move away. I would have never gone outside of my apartment, if it hadn't been for you," he told her.

"And never would have been put in danger," she teased.

"Yeah," Winston said thoughtfully as he once again held her out where he could see her. "Thanks for that too. I think I needed a little danger."

"Hey, don't hog the Dory," Raleigh mused as he pulled her into his own appreciative hug. "Thanks for saving my life."

"Thanks for saving mine," she told him. As she pulled back, she straightened his shirt and commanded, "Be good."

"Hey, you know me," Raleigh responded with a wink of his eye. For a glimpse of a second, his expression turned serious. "You know, it would be easier for me to be good if I had a friend around to referee me and kick me when I'm being a jerk."

Dory swallowed hard, realizing that she was actually holding back tears. She couldn't reply to Raleigh's words, but she managed a nod of understanding.

Moving to the last of the three, Dory waited for a long while before she lifted her fogged eyes to face his eerie silver eyes. He was rubbing the back of his neck nervously and he appeared to be fretting over some word that was suffocating him.

In a swift motion, Dory leaned up to Ghost's ear and whispered, "Good luck. If you remember me after you get your new life, then look me up."

He pulled her into a tight hug. His embrace was chilly and Dory did her best not to shudder. "I won't forget," he promised.

Before Dory could question how long it would be before she could see her friends again, Gilda summoned the imps. They carried away each of men back through Gilda's apartment and back to their homes. Winston waved at her from his awkward position of being carried under his armpits, legs, and back by a dozen imps. Raleigh grinned at Dory, his fangs flashing in the light of the stairway. Ghost squeezed Dory's fingers one last time and quickly added, "I'll miss you." Dory did not answer. She turned back up the stairs and returned to the roof before the imps carried Ghost away.

Gilda approached her and wiped a tear gently from Dory's face. She then set the droplet upon one of her lilies. "What have you decided upon for your lease?" she asked nonchalantly as if the young woman had not just been close to crying.

Wiping at her dry face, checking for anymore tears, Dory answered with thoughts of her new friends. "I was wondering, what if my contract was open ended. I could have the freedom to move out whenever I wished. What do you say to that?" She figured her proposal was a long shot, but if there was one thing Dory had most certainly learned was that asking never hurt anyone.

Gilda lifted up a shiny silver watering can and began to fuss over a bed of amaryllis. Minutes passed silently as she sprinkled water over the sturdy leaves and bright colors. Dory waited patiently, her legs aching from all of her adventures and her head still throbbing with her earlier injury.

At last, Dory asked politely, "Would you like to work out something else? I can understand if you don't want to agree to that deal. You are trying to run a business here. Leasing apartments is considered a business, right?"

Gilda stood upright, blinking her eyes innocently at Dory. She then smiled and responded with utter astonishment. "My dear girl, I already made the deal with you. If you wish an open contract, then you shall have an open contract. I'm not even certain why we are still discussing this. Go home."

With a beaming grin, Dory bobbed her legs as if to curtsy to the woman. "Thank you!" She turned to leave, and then thought about the many flights of stairs and monsters awaiting her. Turning back to Gilda, Dory asked, "Why didn't you have the imps take me home also?"

"I do not want the imps going that far south in the building and finding out there are more humans living here besides you," Gilda clarified with nothing but good intentions in her tone. "Besides, you have another way to get home."

"I don't really want to go back through the building by myself," Dory admitted.

Gilda took a moment to lean over Frank and rub him on his fuzzy stomach until his left back leg shook before answering. "You can get down to your apartment with no difficulty what so ever. In fact, you've had an easy way through the building all of this time." Gilda stood up and whispered into her ear, "You still have the silver key? I will tell you what few know. This building was made with a single elevator and the only way to work it is with that key."

"I've never seen an elevator," Dory pointed out with annoyance. "And I've been all the way through every floor of this building."

"It stays hidden from those who cannot be trusted

with it. That awful hermit woman who used to have your apartment stole it, and then managed to lose it. That is why her sister wanted it so badly. She could have had power over everyone if she could easily get between floors." Gilda lead her back down into home with Frank taking the stairs two at a time in order to follow.

"You knew about all of that too, huh. Can I ask you, why did the Obnoxious Neighbor shrink like that? I don't have any magic powers or anything. What happened exactly?"

"You stood up to a bully. Bullies tend to melt away when their power is taken from them. Simple as that." They stood in front of the only wall with no photos or art hung upon it. "The key." She held out her palm and without hesitation Dory handed the silver key over to her.

She pressed the key into the wall and a lock formed around the silver object. The wall split and opened. Gilda handed the key back to Dory and motioned to the small square room that was now in the wall. "Simply press the button and do not lose that key. I'm trusting you."

Dory boldly hugged the woman. "Thank you. Thanks for all your help."

She stepped into the elevator. Frank hopped on with her with complete trust. Everything within was silver and in the same art deco design she saw at the front of the building. Two rows of buttons lined the wall to the left of the doors. Pressing down on the number one with a fierce determination, the elevator closed just as Gilda waved at the girl. The elevator sped downward. Dory stood against the wall, bracing herself against the velocity of the little car. Frank curled up tightly in a corner, his ears perking up at the sound of the gears moving around them. Then, within seconds, the car stopped. Dory waited patiently as the doors slid open once again.

Chapter Twenty-Four:
**   The First Floor; Home Again**

Stepping off the elevator and into the hallway, Dory was amazed by how friendly and quaint the entrance to the building seemed. Frank followed her off of the car and the doors slid closed. The elevator vanished into the pattern in the wall; no one would have guessed that the mural was a pair of doors awaiting passengers. Pocketing the silver key with a little smile, Dory took out her apartment key. She went to unlock the door, but paused at the handle.

"C'mon, Frank," she said to the little dog. "We have someone else to see."

She went up the stairs and knocked on the door of the Crazy Cat Lady's apartment. Dory made certain to have a tight hold on Frank. As the door began to crack open, she started to talk excitedly, "Thanks for all of your help before. I've decided to just stick it out and see how things go before I do anything to my lease. I just wanted to tell—"

When the stood fully opened, Dory was faced with a young mother who had two sweet looking children hiding behind her. "I'm sorry, what?" the woman asked kindly.

Dory glanced around the hallway. She was at the right apartment. "Hi," she nervously answered, "I, um . . . I'm sorry. I was looking for the woman that lived here with all the cats."

"You must be mistaken," the mother said with understanding. "We don't have any cats. My son, Tip, is allergic."

"Oh." Dory thought over this for a moment, wondering if she should argue or ask how long the woman had been living in the flat. Instead, she extended out her hand and smiled an honest smile. "Silly me. Must have gotten the number wrong. I'm Dorothea; I live in the apartment below yours."

"Hi there. I'm Maud. This is Tip and Jackie. If any of my kids are ever making too much noise for you, just let me know." One of her sons smiled mischievously as if planning to stomp across the floor just for Dory's annoyance.

Dory sighed, "I'm sure they won't bother me." She continued to grin in awkward silence for several seconds before adding, "Actually, I have a friend named Maud. And if you ever need anything from me, let me know. My apartment is right by the mailboxes. Well, it was nice meeting you."

"Oh yes. Come up and see us again. A lot of the neighbors around here really seem to keep to themselves," Maud said with a twinge of regret.

"I'll do that," Dory responded aloud, while thinking to herself. Before she turned away, she called back, "And Maud, don't ask about the neighbors. You'll get more than you bargained for."

She started back down the stairs, setting Frank onto the floor so he could follow her. "She was gone," she muttered. "Or maybe she was never there." Looking back at the puppy, she bit her lip. "Maybe it really was all a dream and I've lost my mind." The puppy tilted his head to one side with interest. "That's what I thought," she murmured.

She entered her apartment and was thrilled to be surrounded by all of her possessions. Suddenly, she felt the urge to unpack every box, to organize each object, and reminisce the story behind everything she owned. She even hooked up her computer and e-mailed a few of her friends she had not bothered with in a long time.

The next day, she woke up early when a ringing startled her. Dory was happy to be in her bed and tried to savor the moment a little longer until she realized where the ringing was coming from. The cell phone rang furiously from where it was plugged in on the floor. Dory lifted the small device, realizing she's barely noticed how she had been without it for days. "Hello." Her greeting exuded all of her cheer into a single word.

"Dory! Dory, honey, where have you been?" her mother's voice frantically answered. "You're cell phone was off and your father and I have been trying to get a hold of you! I even tried calling your work, but I forgot you had taken the week off—"

"I've been here," she told her mom truthfully. "I was getting to know the neighbors." Looking around her unpacked apartment, she thought for a moment as her mom started on a list of questions.

"Anyone nice? Make any friends? What do they do for a living? Are you feeling safe there? Any cute guys?"

"Yes. Yes. Not sure. Yes. And depends on your definition of cute," Dory explained. "Hey, Mom. I was thinking about doing a housewarming dinner later in the week. Would you and Dad be able to come next Saturday? I'll invite some of my new friends."

The words stunned Dory's mom. "I— Of course, hon. Well, my goodness. You are in a good mood. Are you actually going to cook for this dinner?"

"Yes, Mom," Dory answered with a laugh. "I'll even have the apartment unpacked and cleaned up in time for it. So, six o'clock Friday?"

"Six o'clock," her mom repeated, "I'll bring dessert."

"And Dad?"

"Yes, of course." Her mom's voice had grown quiet and Dory realized she must have been giving her father confused expressions at that moment.

There was a succession of knocks at the door. "Someone's here," she told her mom. "I'll call you later. Love you."

"We love you too," her mother replied followed by a great deal of stunned "ums" as she hung up.

With the phone back to being plugged in, Dory went to answer the door. Raleigh and Winston stood in her hallway, looking out of breath. Her jaw fell in a slackened half, smile-half awe. "Did you guys come to check on me? What happened to the park trip and 'social outings'?" she questioned, attempting to read their furrowed brows. "Not that I'm not happy to see you. I was going to ask if you guys wanted to come over for dinner with my parents. We'll have to make up excuses for why you and Ghost aren't eating, Raleigh, but—" She stood on tip toe and gazed into the hallway behind them. "Where is Ghost? He didn't come with you?"

"That's why we're here," Winston told her frantically. His hands twisted around one another, course hairs beginning to nervously sprout from his skin. "We can't find him."

"He just vanished," Raleigh added.

"He is a ghost. Ghosts do that," she commented.

"This is different." Raleigh rubbed the ruby ring upon his own hand. "Something strange is happening on the fourth floor. They have the stairway closed off and they won't let me into my apartment. There are EMTs and firemen swarming all over the place—"

"And you think that has something to do with Ghost?"

Winston scratched at his hands and the tufts of hair grew a little longer. "We thought maybe he was practicing his powers and there was an accident. If someone was hurt because of Ghost, he— He—"

Raleigh set a hand on Winston's shoulder. "He

probably isn't taking it well. Trouble is we can't get up there to see what is going on."

Dory nodded at them, their worry washing over her. "We'll take the elevator."

"The . . . Wait, what?" both of her friends cried out with a mixture of confusion and irritation as she moved between them into the hallway. Frank followed before she locked her apartment door.

Going to the hidden doors in the wall, Dory used the silver key to open the elevator once again. She, Raleigh, Winston, and Frank piled in. The werewolf kept to the middle of the car with a nervous stance, careful not to touch the silver walls.

Her finger hovered over the lines of buttons. At the back of her mind, a voice fretted at her, begging her not to go to the fourth floor. What if what she found was worse than all of the rest of their week? What if Ghost was gone for good? Still, she forced her hand to move and the number four lit up. They all felt the little tickle in their stomachs as the car shot upwards, then halted with a ding.

They piled out of the elevator, unnoticed by the nosy crowd which had gathered in the hallway. An ambulance gurney sat blocking the door of the apartment belonging to the rude man Dory had met that first day. She hovered close to a smartly dressed woman in her late fifties standing at the edge of her own doorway, cell phone at the ready as if something worse were about to happen.

"Excuse me. What happened?" Dory asked her with a mix of innocence and curiosity.

The woman tapped her mobile phone against her chin. "Do you know the young man that lives there?"

"I've made his acquaintance," Dory answered, not bothering to hide her disgust. "Did he have an accident or something?"

"I don't know. I know he was sick. Didn't see him come

out of his apartment for a while now. Then, this morning I heard him screaming and called the police. The fire department broke in and the medical team has been in there at least thirty minutes now."

"Screaming?" Raleigh repeated.

The woman gave him an intrigued look and tugged at the top button of her blouse. "Yes. Sounded like he was being attacked. I thought there was a burglar." She bat her eyes at Raleigh as she expressed her suspicions.

Dory moved through the hallway, her whole body alert with a panic. Ghost must have been there trying to spook people. Nothing bad could happen to him, she rationalized. He was already dead. What could the awful man do to him?

She could feel Winston's tense hand on her shoulder as he followed close behind. She sensed Raleigh was not too far behind.

Three EMTs exited the door, muttering to one another. "I've never seen anyone make such a fast recovery. I thought he was dead when we got here."

"I still say we should take him to the hospital," a second EMT explained. She started to roll away the gurney and added over her shoulder, "Wish we could force him to go."

"First of all, that's illegal. Secondly, doctors will think we've gone nuts. I couldn't find anything wrong with him after he woke up." The third EMT helped the second as they started to push the gurney down the stairs.

Over the sound of the metal wheels clattering over each step, Dory heard the voice of the young man from the other day. "Thanks," he called to the three medics with grin as he appeared in his apartment entrance. He leaned upon the door frame, allowing his monogrammed night shirt to wrinkle as he crossed his arms.

Dory stopped short. She knew how strange it would be

if she called out for Ghost, yet an uneasy butterfly in the pit of her gut fluttered against her insides.

Winston pulled on her shoulder. "I don't think he's here, Dory. Let's go."

The young man in the doorway stiffened a little at the sight of the vampire, werewolf, and girl. His grin melted. Words escaped him and Raleigh glared in response, not liking the looks of the human.

Dory tried to lock eyes with the rude man, remembering the effort he had used upon her before. She willed herself forward. The man's gaze fell suddenly in uncharacteristic shyness. The lights in the hallway dimmed, flickered, and then went back to full illumination as Dory moved nearer. Winston twitched at the electricity's behavior and Raleigh froze.

Dory finished the long walk across the short hallway. She took the young man's hand. "Ghost?" A part of her new the truth without asking and a part of her was terrified by the thought of him within the body of such an unpleasant man.

Raleigh squinted at him to try and see the spirit within. "You did it. You actually did it?"

As if suddenly feeling the need to justify his actions, Ghost explained quickly, his mannerism shining through the muscles of his new body. "I went to scare him and found he was dying. So I thought—"

Winston wrung his hands. "Do you think any of his friends will notice? Are you going to have to be him now?"

"I've been going through his stuff and I don't think he had a lot of friends. I couldn't help it. I saw the opportunity and I took it. And if Gilda still wants me to be the new landlord, then I won't have to work his crumby job." He gulped and hung his head. "I suppose I shouldn't stay. It probably isn't right. What do you think, Dory?"

She watched as the neighbors retreated back into

their homes, the excitement over. She rubbed her thumb across the alien hand of the body Ghost occupied, briefly sensing the cool touch of the spirit who sat with her in the dark. She recognized the admiring look within his eyes, the cool silver-blue still visible despite the original shade the rude man's eyes had been. With a squeeze of his new hand in hers, she answered, "I think—" A relieved grin broke across her face. "Welcome home."

Acknowledgments:
Scott P. "Doc" Vaughn for graphic arts help (and for letting me borrow that one book which you probably forgot that I still have)
Kane Gilmour for hours on the phone listening to stupid questions
KAD Creations for the cover art
Patrick Kennedy for help with the ending
Tom Dushku for the technical assistance
And Rachel Woodruff for the deviled eggs.

Megan E. Vaughn became a writer to distract from the fact that she does not know how to read. She has been locked in an epic battle with dust bunnies ever since she moved from Wisconsin to Arizona as a child. Beyond that, she has earned her degree in history, traveled to many historical ruins in various places, and forced her friends to pretend to be impressed by historically significant rocks. Currently she lives. . .right behind you! Ha! Made you look!

www.ingramcontent.com/pod-product-compliance
Lightning Source LLC
Chambersburg PA
CBHW021011120726
47905CB00009B/2963